EXHALE WITH INTENT

by Brett Cimino

Published by Brett Cimino

EXHALE WITH INTENT

ISBN-13: 978-0-692-68406-1

Cover art by
Eric Scopelliti
Graphics by Xavier Bland for Design Your Ink
designyourink@gmail.com

Published by
Brett Cimino

Visit **Exhale With Intent's** websites at
www.exhalewithintent.com
www.facebook.com/ExhaleWithIntent
instagram.com/exhalewithintentbook

Printing history
First edition published in April 2016

Artwork "Steve K" painted by Dominic Cimino

Dedication

Because of my father's free spirit and dedication to the arts, I was able to appreciate and get involved with that freedom myself from a young age. The visual conception that takes place in the creation of my expressions is what is most important to me. Thank you, Dad, for always supporting me and listening to me whenever I needed it.

Exhale With Intent is dedicated to all branches of the United States military and to the men and women who protect this great country.

Chapter 1

Afghanistan—September 2005

I look out the dusty window of the gun truck I have been living out of for the past few months and think about my guys, who are getting blown to shit. I, too, have had a pocketful of close calls that keep me up most nights, along with some of the shit that I've had to push down my gullet. The lifeless bodies stacked up in my mind drive me crazy if I think about them for too long.

The brakes squeal, crying out their abrupt stop, and yank me from my thoughts. The short, camouflaged convoy parks in front of the address that's on the wanted poster for today. Marco, a ranking officer, got a last-minute tip from a two-bit informant who gave up this location for homegrown IEDs. Tips like these can sometimes backfire, but usually pan out to be fairly solid. Our group has been chosen to check this location and use whatever force we need, and if deemed necessary, take them out.

I watch my guys, parked in front of us, step out of the three-ton turtleback and look around the desert. It's like any other day, a monotonous, scorching, drab, tan-colored dust bowl. I glance at the new guys riding with our infantry team this week. These guys have only been in-country about a month, but are assisting us today not only to accompany our group and keep a watch out, but also to recruit some young talent. In two months, it will be my tenth year in the Corps, and my seventh with special ops.

We have snipers watching this mission because of the large number of IED fatalities. They're set up in a building southeast of us. It's more like half of a building, thanks to the bombing that took place last week. They sit roughly a thousand meters away doing what they do best: being invisible.

The disheveled property that is today's target is surrounded by a wall with a gate that's twisted and smashed, but locked up tight. I gaze around at what's left of a small commuter bus that's flipped on its side, along with the charred skeletons of scattered cars. Jackson, our radio man, wipes a heavy bead of sweat from his brow and hops on the net to reach out to the sniper team for intel on whether this assignment is cool or hot. I adjust my Kevlar as we wait for a green light from our third eye before pushing past the point of no return. The sniper team responds back: zero activity since taking post late last night. However, Rick, a veteran sniper I trained under in sniper school, informs us there's a large collection of propane tanks located on the right side of the building.

These types of search missions are very difficult. We fight in backyards, among families and small children. Al Qaeda has a funny way of sculpting themselves into backyard picnic-basket innocents, making it pretty much impossible to distinguish a local bystander from an enemy combatant. It's a tough and dangerous situation when you don't know who you're fighting.

"Sarge, Rick said you owe him a case of beer," Jackson says with a smirk.

I squeeze the bolt cutters against my chest and shear the lock in half before Jackson can put his radio away. "That old ass-in-the-grass will hold me to that case of beer till I die." I kick open the gate and enter onto the property.

It looks and smells like a dirty toilet bowl. I scan the premises and watch over my platoon, trying to put eyes on the situation and in the back of my head. The LP tanks Rick spotted are near a flimsy metal shed in the back of the building, built into the corner of the abutting property's fence. There have to be two dozen 20-pound tanks piled up, hiding under dirty, torn vinyl tops and weighed down by broken-up pallets. The present find makes me think that our tip-off was right on— this is definitely a homegrown bomb factory.

"Sergeant, over here," Williams, our point man, calls out as he approaches the side door of this shithole with extreme caution.

Our mission is only half over. We need to secure the entire area and remove all possible bomb-making equipment from the premises. I follow along with the platoon, one behind the other, zigzagging in single file. We cut off at five deep, leaving the rest of the men outside to hold our cover for any close-quarter surprises.

We enter what was once a kitchen and get slammed with a smell that almost takes me to my knees. My guys struggle with the foul odor, but they stay in the game, focused, trained, and ready for anything. I round the corner with my rifle leading the way and scan the next room through my sight. I turn quickly, scanning the area, trying to find the source of this familiar sound. I hear birds singing and see them perched atop a filthy lampshade sitting by itself in the opposite corner of the dreary room . . .

~~~

Providence, Rhode Island—September 2013

The sunlight that glared through the window stung my eyes as I pried them open. I rolled over and whacked the button on my alarm clock, which had woken me up from the dream that still haunted me most nights. It was time that I dragged my ass out of bed and got ready for work.

My name is Elliot Frantallo. I was a thirty-five-year-old Providence police detective when all this went down. I rented an apartment on the east side of the city with my fiancée, Megan Wilson, who was a branch manager for a local credit union.

After a shower and a quick breakfast, I was out the door and off to work. I walked toward my unmarked car, getting a nose full of coffee aroma that wafted through the early morning air. Jasper's, a small but popular breakfast nook that sat a diagonal block away, grabbed at my senses just about every morning. I rounded the corner into the driveway to get my daily espresso-like good-morning cheer from my landlord, retired Providence police captain Jack Pollenso. He had better than thirty years on me, but you'd swear he was in his mid-fifties. Jack stood tall and muscular at six foot two, with thick salt-and-pepper hair he wore waxed and pulled straight back. He had strong Italian features and roots that fed off Italian soil.

I approached the table on his front porch, where he could be found sitting almost any hour of the day. "Morning, Jack. How you doing?"

Jack smiled and put down his coffee mug. "I'm doing good, kiddo. Will I see ya later for a beer?"

"Sure, that sounds good. Oh, shit! Not tonight. Megan's coming home."

"That's right . . . We've been having so much fun, I forgot. It totally slipped my mind." Jack folded up his morning read and slapped it on the table.

I looked at my watch. I was already running behind.

"Good morning, boys," our neighbor Janice said as she strolled past us.

Janice Smith, a newly single real estate agent in her late forties, lived on John Street and walked by at least twice a day, flaunting all the right curves. She wore her hair in a funky, choppy red-and-caramel bob that always pulled Jack away from whatever he was doing.

Jack's brow pointed to the sky. "Morning, Janice."

I held up my hand with a smile and watched as she and Jack undressed one another with their eyes. "Jack, I really gotta go."

"I know, I know. I get all hung up when she walks by. I can't help it."

"If I were you, I'd be doing the same thing."

Jack laughed and picked up his paper. "We've been on a good tear, Elliot. We'll pick up again tomorrow night." Jack reopened the morning paper with a smirk and got back to what was what.

"Oh, Jack, I almost forgot. I have the rent check on my fridge. I forgot to grab it on my way out."

Jack waved away my concern and drew his *Providence Journal* back into focus.

Chapter 2

I pulled away, watching Jack through the window as he leafed through the paper and sipped his Italian double. Jack had decided that he'd had enough, and resigned the year before. It hadn't been the forty-two years of dealing with all the animals in this city that had pushed him out the door. The political changes within the department had burned him out.

"It's like having a rusted-on nut, and your job is to take it off," he had told me at the time. "So you open your toolbox, and it's full of plastic wrenches. What do you do? You do what you're told, right? You go at it, pulling and tugging on that fused-up pain in the ass. After about fifteen minutes, every fucking wrench in the box is broken and lying on the floor. Well, it's pretty frustrating knowing you could accomplish the job with the right tools, but the tools have all been stripped away."

When Jack left the department, it lost one of its main arteries. Jack was one of the few guys who'd had his finger on the pulse of the city. It's impossible to replace that kind of knowledge and experience, but I guess nothing ever stays the same.

Jack and I had become good friends and had a lot in common. We'd bonded on his front porch, eating great food, getting drunk, and sharing the stories that our eyes had experienced and our hearts would never, ever forget.

I swung a right on Benefit Street, passing by houses that were mostly full of Brown University and Rhode Island School of Design students. I pushed in a tape of the big hits of the '80s. I kept it in the deck for morning commutes, when stations were just talk, talk, and more talk. I couldn't bear to listen to that early morning radio bullshit they stuffed down everyone's throats. Some people said I was a negative bastard when I'd talk like that, but I really didn't give a shit what anyone thought and would continue to follow my old-school principles.

I banged a left and rode the brake down College Hill, with the '80s flowing into the clean morning air. I enjoyed the early morning commute to work, because it was usually before every pore in the city got clogged up. A couple of RISD kids walked beside my car as I was stopped at a red light where Benefit and South Angell connect. These kids were definitely '80s fans. They signaled a thumbs-up while walking by in their funky, artistic wardrobes and multicolored hair.

We're always taught that the simple stuff in life trumps all. Just the freedom and experience of driving in to work or walking to school are worth more than any amount of money in the world, and anyone who's been in a really bad spot in their life, or on their deathbed, knows what I mean.

Megan had been visiting her sister for the past week, up on her family's farm in the uppermost corner of western Massachusetts. Her sister, Denise, was all she had left in her immediate family. Both parents had passed away in the past two years, which had been extremely hard on Megan and Denise. It had been tough to sleep without Megan in bed next to me, but I could remember saying the opposite when she'd moved in and started hogging all the covers. It's hard to break a routine, and also hard to break into one.

When I had decided to turn the page and start a new chapter, and left the Marines, it was the most difficult decision I'd dealt with in my entire life. It also very well may have been the reason I was still alive. So I guess sometimes breaking a routine, whether it's on a negative note or a positive one, can work to your advantage.

Traffic on 95 had started to pile up by the time I reached the station. After shooting the shit with a couple of guys outside the entrance who had just moved to third shift, I entered the complex and got to my desk. I immediately jumped on a report that was past due.

I had been grinding away at the report for a couple of hours when I got a text from Megan that she was home and in bed, naked and waiting. Megan always knew how to motivate me to get my ass in gear and get home to her.

I looked at the clock and realized I needed to slow down my pulse, with over five hours to go before I could leave. I was thinking of sailing a mouthful of coffee into my trash basket and going home sick with the "flu," when my Irish compadre appeared at my desk like a cloud on a beach day.

Sean Kelley stood in front of me throwing around his hands, and then took off in a big hustle, continuing to mumble as he walked away from my desk. Sean stood five eleven and wore his hair short on the sides and combed over to the right on top. He was a mild guy who needed his buttons firmly pounded on to set him off.

"C'mon, Elliot, we gotta go!" Sean hollered as he rounded the corner and disappeared from sight.

I guessed everyone would miss my morning puke act, and Megan would have to miss me shedding my clothes—at least for now. I grabbed my coat off the back of my chair and rolled into a sprint to catch up to Sean.

I finally got within talking distance. "So what's up?"

Sean power walked over and around a small series of puddles on the way to the car. "There's been a triple murder over on the South Side."

What else is new, I thought to myself. I was actually eager for a fresh case. I needed something more exciting than the crap that had been dumped on my desk lately.

"Why don't you drive, Elliot?" Sean opened the door and grabbed shotgun. "I'd like to finish my coffee. I'll tell you what I know on the way."

"Yeah, sure, no problem." I fired up the blue unmarked and left the back lot, heading for the South Side.

Sean filled me in on what little he knew as we drove up Elmwood Ave to the murder scene. "Apparently, the owner of the three-tenement house works maintenance over at the hospital, third shift. Guy comes home this morning and decides to do a load of laundry. Goes down to the cellar and just about has a heart attack when he almost trips over his tenants, who were not only dead down there, but from what I've heard, carved up pretty bad, too."

"Wow, that's a beautiful way to start the day, huh?"

Sean chuckled under his breath and sipped his coffee. "Oh, yeah, wonderful."

Sean and I partnered on some of the bigger cases. He'd been with the department for fifteen years, and when he first got into Dicks, had actually worked a few cases with Jack.

Murder in the city was gradually rising. In the almost eight years that I had been on the department, I'd seen a huge change. The job was definitely not normal, but then again, neither was my first job. I'd gone from fighting a war overseas to fighting one right here in my backyard. Too many days of not being able to tell the good guys from the bad guys and never knowing if a gun would end up at my head because I had turned my back on the wrong mutt. I had definitely learned never to let my guard down.

We pulled up to the house. There was already a crowd on the sidewalk. The majority of them hung over the fence like animals waiting to get fed at the zoo.

"What the fuck," I said. "It's the same shit every time. I wish these people would just go home." I threw the car in park and looked at the faceless crowd that circled around the frontage of the murder scene.

Sean shook his head. "Let's check out the crime scene before we talk to the owner. We'll catch him on the way out."

We got out of the car and cut across the lawn in the backyard, trying to avoid the commotion and bullshit carnival act that was lingering around the front. Some brass was already there. Whenever there's a death, some of the big boys have to show up to deal with all the political bullshit.

Sean and I stood on the landing and ducked down the basement stairs. I was briefly blinded by the drastic change of stepping into darkness. Halfway down the rickety, squeaky, slanted staircase, the lingering aroma of death slapped us in the face. Forensics was already there working, with Lieutenant Jimmy Taylor as the lead man collecting evidence. Not much got by Jimmy. He had eyes like twin telescopes, and his attention to detail was far superior to anyone's I'd seen in this department.

"Whatcha got for us, Jimmy?" My pupils adjusted and dialed in as my feet safely leveled off on the concrete floor.

"Three males. One African American, two Caucasians. No forced entry. We're picking up prints everywhere, but I have a feeling our perp wore gloves." Jimmy's eyes shifted as Sean stepped down to the landing behind me. "Hey, Sean, what's going on?"

Jimmy and Sean had been good friends and drinking buddies longer than I'd been a cop.

"Not much, Jimmy," Sean said.

Sean and I checked the three bodies, which were lying in a pile in front of a small workbench. The bench didn't have many tools on it, but it had a lot of blood, already dried and covered by flies. They buzzed around the basement like little fighter jets.

"Holy shit," Sean said. "These guys are fucked up."

We all stared for a moment, studying the condition of the three corpses. Even if we'd had any run-ins with these joes prior to this, visual identification was definitely out of the question.

I took a closer look at the brutality, but also the precision, of these murders. The specific yet gruesome job was probably the most heinous I'd ever seen without a bomb having gone off. "It looks like these guys were tortured."

"Oh, absolutely," Jimmy stated. "This trio took a monster beating, and then our perp took a stiletto or some type of bayonet-style knife and inserted it into each of the three victims' ears and bottomed out the steel. My guess, that's what did them in, but the autopsy should determine that." Jimmy pointed out the deep bruising on their bodies where they'd been beaten before their deaths.

I took a few steps back. "So, wait a minute, let me get this right. What you're saying is one guy did all this fucking damage?" I didn't disagree with Jimmy's assumption, but I was having a hard time swallowing it.

"That's exactly what I'm saying."

Sean and Jimmy looked at me and then continued to move forward with the three John Does. I walked around the basement, looking for any loose end that might have been waiting to get picked up. I didn't see anything out of the ordinary, but I was processing the fact that we had a big fucking problem on our hands if one man had done all this damage, and all in one sitting.

I ducked under the old steam piping that was still covered with air cell and asbestos insulation and about an inch of dust. I made my way over to the center chimney, where the old black-and-white snowman boilers were located that were probably original to the house. The enormous chestnut beam that ran down the middle of the cellar sat on huge blue cement columns that were covered in graffiti, along with the blood that was spattered across two of them.

"Jimmy, are you sure just one perp is responsible?" I asked, hoping he might have changed his forecast in the past two minutes.

Jimmy looked at me with that shit-eating grin he wore so well. "I know it's hard to believe, but the exact same technique was used on each victim. We're not dealing with a first-timer or some drug deal gone bad." He ripped into a coconut jelly stick with complete confidence.

I overlooked the basement fiasco. "Gotta be military. Or some highly trained psycho."

"Maybe it was one of those red-assed monkeys that busted outta Roger Williams Zoo." Sean's relaxed fist covered his immediate outburst.

We all looked at each other and burst out laughing at Sean's scenario.

"Oh yeah, a baboon," Jimmy said. "Those things are vicious." A piece of doughnut fell from the corner of his mouth and onto one of the stiffs.

"Maybe they were drugged," I said.

Sean sipped his coffee and looked at me with his brow raised. "Now that's a possibility."

Between the nasty smell that was pouring off these guys and the brain matter on the floor, I was itching for some fresh air and looked to the stairwell.

"Anything's possible, but it's highly unlikely," Jimmy commented.

Frank Crager, Jimmy's sidekick, and his second set of hands and eyes, unzipped a navy blue gym bag and opened it up. "Hey guys, check this out. There must be at least a hundred pounds of crystal meth in here."

"Where the hell did that come from?" I asked.

"It was underneath this last body." Frank pointed to the stiff who had been on the bottom of the pile.

Now this just doesn't make any sense, unless we're dealing with a vigilante or something, I thought to myself. "Why would someone leave that much street value behind?"

"That might just be the question of the day," Jimmy said.

Sean looked at me and shrugged his shoulders.

At that point, I just wanted to get out of there. "We should call vice to see if they can plug us in with any possible dealers who could be responsible for this much product."

Sean nodded. "My first pick? That prick Eddie Gomez."

"Either him or that scumbag Joel Ferguson." I shook Jimmy's and Frank's hands and headed for the daylight at the top of the stairs. "Come on," I said to Sean. "Let's go see what the owner knows."

I flipped the light switch at the bottom of the dark, winding staircase and got no response. I looked up at the antique fixture. It hung from a bundled-up ball of wires that was held together with black tape. Some of the wires poked through broken lath boards where the horsehair plaster was missing. I shook my head and looked to my right, where I spotted a flashlight hanging from a nail on the side of a floor joist. I reached up and grabbed it, flipped the switch forward, and lit up the dark exit.

The crooked staircase had worn-out treads and chopped-up kickplates, and the busted banister was held up with a paint can and some old bricks. The top and probably tenth coat of paint was bright green and super shiny, making it easy to detect the dark spot five steps up.

I shined a light on it and took a closer look, confirming my suspicion that the dark spatter was definitely blood. "Jimmy, over here. Could be our perp's." I laid the flashlight down on the same step, leaving it to shine on the new evidence as we left the dungeon behind.

Sean and I walked to the front of the house, where Major Mitch Sullivan was talking to the owner on the front walkway.

Sean looked at me. "So what do you think?"

"I don't know," I said. "Maybe vigilante."

"I didn't think of that."

Sean and I whispered back and forth and kept our pace toward the next situation slow, trying to keep any speculations we had under our hats.

Chapter 3

"Ah, Mr. Martinez," Major Sullivan said. "These are the detectives I was telling you about, Kelley and Frantallo. They'll be handling this case, and will help you with whatever you need."

Sean and I shook hands with Mr. Martinez.

The major handed Mr. Martinez his card. "Please, call me if you need anything." He shook the landlord's hand and excused himself.

Major Mitch Sullivan was a decorated officer who had been with Providence Police for thirty-eight years. He was a respected officer who had a lot of clout within the department and also with the mayor's office. He'd worked with Jack on some big cases back in the day and still had a close relationship with him, which worked in my favor. He had pulled me out of some tight jams.

Sean sent off a text before sliding his phone into his jacket pocket. "Mr. Martinez, before we get started, what's your first name?"

"Victor," the landlord replied quickly and with a heavy Spanish accent. He lit a twisted, squashed-up, bent cigarette from a crumpled and now empty soft pack that he crushed in his hand and chucked onto the front porch. Still dressed in his work uniform, he looked around at all the confusion as if the whole world was coming down on top of him.

I made my way up the front steps and took stock. The screen door was ready to fall off, wires hung out of the siding where the doorbell was attached, and the storm windows were so built up with dust and dirt that you could barely see the cheap, broken blinds that hung just inches behind the thick, dingy film.

"Victor, why don't you start by bringing us up to the apartment these guys were renting from you?" I said.

Martinez took a long drag from his cigarette and looked at the hot ash. "Actually, Detective, Slim was the only one who lived here. I don't really know who the other two guys are."

"Which one is Slim?"

"The skinny colored boy."

Sean looked up at the aluminum-sided soffit that was popped open and had yellow jackets coming and going from it like traffic at a four-way intersection. "Have you ever seen the other two guys that are down there with him?"

"Of course. They come around a lot, but don't hang around too long. I don't know what they do, man. I'm just happy to get my rent every month."

"We understand, Victor," Sean said. "Don't stress out. But the more you remember, the better chance we have of nailing this guy."

"I know, Detective. I'm trying."

"Can you think of anyone who'd want to kill these guys?" I asked. "Any recent fights or arguments? Any type of dispute?" I looked out at the crowd of bystanders, still gawking and still growing by the rusty, silver spray-painted chain-link fence.

Martinez fanned through his keys for the first-floor door. "No, nothing like that, but there has been a much older guy hanging with them just recently. The guy's bad news, man." He fiddled with the lock, turned the key, and pushed the door to the apartment open.

"Can you describe what he looks like?" I asked.

Martinez pulled out a new pack of Reds and yanked the gold seal on the cellophane wrapper, opening it. "Of course. White guy, probably late sixties. He wears a baseball cap, pulled down low, like this." He pulled his Red Sox cap down, imitating the guy's stance. "Oh, one more thing. He's one mean-looking son of a bitch."

I could see in his eyes that Martinez was scared of this older man. "Does he have any distinguishing marks? Tattoos?"

"A limp?" Sean cut in, anxious from the smell of death that lingered around the residence. "Anything that might set him apart in a lineup."

"Oh, yeah, a scar on his ear and on his cheek." Martinez rubbed the side of his face and earlobe with his thumb, and the ash of his half-smoked cigarette butt fell onto his shoulder. The skinny, chain-smoking landlord had a face full of pockmarks and a heavy crop of blackheads along his neckline.

"What the fuck," I said, poking my head through the doorway. "This apartment is a friggin' dump." That may have been an understatement. Slim's apartment looked like a decade-old war zone, full of neglect, clutter, and filth that greeted us with not only the sight of it all, but also a scent that would gag a hog at chow time.

"I didn't know he lived this bad," Martinez said, looking at the filth. "I haven't been in here in probably a year."

Sean, uninterested in the cleanliness of the apartment, cut right to the chase. "It really doesn't matter. Forget about that. Just tell us more about this older guy."

Martinez leaned up against the refrigerator, next to a stack of porn magazines that consumed a small butcher-block kitchen cart hugged tight against the right side of the fridge. "About a week ago, I went downstairs to grab my laundry, and there they were, all of them, hanging down near my workbench. Slim and the others said hi to me, but that guy looked at me like . . . He had this look on his face, and in his eyes, that made me freeze up like ice." Martinez got more nervous and fumbled his words around. "I could tell that he didn't like me being down there, you know? He looked at me so bad, man, like he wanted me to go kill myself or something. He has a power that I can't explain. Back home, we'd call him *diablo blanco*." His hand trembled. He took the last filtered drag from his cigarette and ran it under the kitchen faucet.

"White devil," I said.

"Yes, that's right." Martinez turned my way. "This guy . . . He's bad news, man. I've seen men like this in my country. They have all the power and money." Martinez threw the wet butt into the trash bin, which was full to the top and overflowing.

"Listen, why don't you come downtown and work with our sketch artist?" Sean suggested.

Martinez checked the time on his wristwatch that he wore on his inner arm a few inches higher than normal. "Sure, Detective. Okay."

I popped my head into Slim's bedroom and got a whiff of damp, moldy laundry. The sheets on the bed were all twisted up and stained in three or four different earth-toned shades. "What did Slim do for work?"

"I don't know. He always paid me in cash and was never late." Martinez stared at the dirty clothes and shit-stained underwear piled up in the corner of the kitchen. "I can tell you one thing—nobody around here messed with these guys."

Sean and I look at each other, wondering who their guardian angel might have been.

"Did he have a girlfriend or any lady companions?" Sean asked.

I looked at Sean, thinking that had to have been the dumbest question. I wondered how a girl would even step foot into this shithole.

"That boy had a different girl every month," Martinez said. "I couldn't keep up."

"Did these girls wear dark glasses and walk with a stick?" I quipped. "Maybe a dog by their side . . . German Shepard?"

Sean bellowed out a good chuckle.

"What glasses?" Martinez asked, confused by my sarcasm. He skimmed through a *Hustler*. "They were hookers, I think."

"I hope he tipped them good," I said.

Sean smirked. "Come on, let's finish this downtown. Actually, Mr. Martinez, just hop in with us. We'll save you the trip and your gas."

We stepped out of the apartment and into the fresh air once again.

"I don't know about you, but I feel like I'm getting bit." I slapped the back of my neck and looked at my hand to see if there was a bug squashed in my palm.

"Will these guys lock up my place for me when they're done?" Martinez asked.

We assured him that once everyone was finished with his house, it would get locked up.

Martinez nodded. "Okay, guys. I go."

We got to the cruiser, and Sean opened the back passenger-side door for Martinez. I turned the key and fired up all eight cylinders.

The tired landlord pulled his door closed. "Can I smoke in here, Detectives?"

"Sure, dude," Sean said. "Just roll down the window." He flipped his finger over his shoulder and pointed to the back window.

I got a whiff of sulfur and cigarette smoke as he lit up and took a drag. He whipped his match out the window. I pulled off the curb in the backyard near a decrepit grapevine and banged a left onto Wood Street. There was still a big gathering of nose bags on the sidewalk, waiting for the dead bodies to appear.

"Hey, guys?" Martinez asked. "How long do you think this is gonna ta—"

Boom!

"What the fuck was that?" Sean turned around, hopping onto his seat with one knee.

I looked into the rearview mirror and saw half of Victor Martinez's head splattered on the back window and running down the vinyl seat. Sean's expression as he observed the mess said it all. I pulled the door handle and threw my door open while simultaneously stomping on the brake pedal and throwing the car into park. I yelled to Sean to follow me. He flew over the driver's seat like Superman, dived out the door, and rolled out onto the concrete. We sat on the sidewalk with our backs leaned up against the car.

Major Sullivan and Sergeant Riggs came running over and crouched down next to us, staying below the outline of the cruiser. Riggs, a veteran street cop, had better than twenty-five years with Providence. He stood somewhere around five feet ten inches and was slightly overweight, with a bald head and a neck as big as a Rottweiler's. I'd heard that he was a nasty bastard, and that the South Side crews didn't fuck with him.

"Are you guys okay?" Sullivan asked.

"We're fine, Major. But he's not." I signaled my thumb to the backseat, where our only witness lay with a big hole in his head.

"Yeah, we saw that . . . My God! This is such a fucking nightmare. Where the hell did that come from?"

"I don't know," I said, "but I'm pretty sure he's done shooting."

I knew what this was. It wasn't some gangbanger turf thing we were dealing with. This guy was a professional sniper, someone military trained. I glanced over the hood of the car for any obvious locations of where the shot might have come from. I couldn't see anything at all with just raw eyeballs. He could've been a dime away, cuddled up in some attic, laughing at us. Our patrolmen were running around in a frenzy, not knowing how to deal with this. They were racing up and down the streets like fucking lunatics.

Sean, still in shock, had his gun drawn, ready for a battle. "How far away do you think he is?"

"I don't know," I said, "but I do know one thing."

"What's that?" Sean replied.

"Our job just went from being dangerous to being suicide."

The four of us leaned up against the car, still wondering if any one of us could end up this guy's bull's-eye out there on the front lawn. All the gawkers at the fence had scattered like rats, disappearing back into the woodwork and out of sight.

I knew the cruisers racing around had a job to do, but I also knew they were going to come up empty-handed. "Everyone's wasting their time."

Sergeant Riggs looked at me with doubt in his eyes. "How can you be so sure they're not going to grab him?"

"Because there are just some things you learn about professional hits like this one. Plus the fact that there are hundreds of buildings around here, and a guy who just pulled off a one-in-a-million shot is probably not going to be walking down the street with the word *guilty* stamped on his forehead." The small chip that Riggs wore on his shoulder, along with this mess that I was no stranger to, got under my skin immediately.

"Are we going to conduct this investigation on your opinion, Detective?" Riggs snapped. "How long have you been a cop?"

Major Sullivan looked at Riggs, knowing he had to nip this in the bud right away. "Sergeant, I want to inform you that the detective whose opinion you're questioning was a special ops marine who has been a sniper for our government. He also turned down a job with the

CIA because he wanted a somewhat normal life, which he now may be regretting. I think we can trust a judgment call from him."

"Hey, I didn't know, Major. I've never read his file. I'm sorry, okay?" Riggs remorsefully shook my hand with his apology.

"Listen, the last thing I want to do is run around the department having a dick-measuring contest. I'm no better than anyone else here, but there are certain things I know, and I know what this is." I explained myself to my small audience and stood up in plain view to untangle my suspicions. "First of all, this guy's a full-blown sniper, and second, that shot came from all of a grand away. The bullet that killed this poor bastard, who was probably our strongest witness, is a three-thirty-eight or equivalent. Believe me, this guy is in a league that only consists of a handful of soldiers. Their training teaches them how not to get caught. Just because this guy can see another kill, and maybe even taste it, he won't grab for it right away. One shot, one kill."

"Well, it sounds like we have a big problem on our hands." Sullivan said.

Patrol cruisers were still weaving through the neighborhood like hornets buzzing around a smashed-up nest that had been whacked out of a tree.

Jimmy and Frank pulled out of the basement and moved into the backseat, where Victor Martinez lay with a big hole in his melon. Rescue tripled on-site when the call went over the radio that a police cruiser had been hit. I stood there, involved with the commotion created by the unknown gunman, thinking that what had been dropped in our lap was not only lead-filled, but also a big paperwork pain in the ass. I looked out and scanned the area, wondering where in the city this madman could be hiding, and what exactly his motive was.

Chapter 4

I realized Sean and I needed to catch a ride back to the station. "We're going to need some wheels, seeing as our ride has become a crime scene."

"Yeah. Once Jimmy retrieves the plug that tore through Martinez's head, they'll wash her out and you'll get your ride back."

Sean and I hopped in with Major Sullivan, and we took off toward the station.

"Hopefully, the lab will come back with some kind of lead for us," Sullivan said. He hooked a left on Broad Street and eyed Sean in his rearview mirror.

"Let's just hope our perp slipped up and got sloppy." I glanced at Mitch Sullivan sitting beside me and hoped that I wouldn't still be doing this shit when I was his age. I looked back at Sean. "Do we have any junk rides in impound?"

"Yeah, I think we have a few shit boxes at Lou's off Admiral."

I turned back to Sullivan with a change of plans. "Hey, Major, can you drop us at Lou's Garage?"

"Sure." Sullivan looked at me and then at Sean with the whites of his eyes blazing, wondering what was on the agenda.

~~~

Lou's Garage was our favorite of several contracted impound sites because Lou was straight out of his mind. We jumped out at the curb and thanked Sullivan for the lift.

He rolled down the window before taking off. "No crazy shit, guys, okay? The media's already foaming at the mouth with the everyday garbage we can't keep up with." Sullivan glared out the window as if we were a couple of teenagers who had the whole house to ourselves, then blew a U-turn and disappeared from sight into the concrete jungle.

We cruised the lot for the perfect beater. I saw a late-model Maxima, but it was a little too flashy for my style. I wanted to wear a mask, something that would blend into the dirty corners and stain-covered city streets. Then I spotted a late-'80s Mustang GT with smoked-out windows, faded paint, and a smashed-up front quarter, parked tight between the garage and the abutting apartment building. "Sean, let's grab that Mustang."

"Let me see what I can do. I'll be right back."

While Sean walked into the service garage to see our buddy Lou, I took advantage of the couple of free minutes and called Megan.

She answered the phone on the first ring. "You missed your chance, my friend."

"You're really hosing me, man. I should've just stayed in bed today."

Megan picked up on my dull riff. "What's wrong, babe?"

"Just another day at work. Don't really have the time to get into it right now."

"Well, I'll be here when you get home."

Her raspy little voice, along with her signature giggle, turned my main sprocket forward again, making me grin.

Sean walked out of the left service bay.

"I gotta go, babe," I said. "I'll see you later."

"Please be careful. I love you."

"I love you, too. 'Bye." I clipped my phone back in its case as Sean handed me the keys to the busted-up, smoked-out, blue-and-gray hatchback.

On the ride back through the South Side, I spouted out some of my thoughts and speculations about our perp while Sean ate a spinach pie he had grabbed back at the garage.

"How is it?" I asked.

Sean whipped a big chunk of dough out the window and onto the sidewalk. "Not enough spinach."

"Cheap bastards. I hate that."

We ran in from the southwest corner, entering the ass end of where I believed the sniper had taken his shot. I'd guessed his exit had been mapped out slicker than shit, so we zoned in to the regular spots and the usual critters who made up the woodwork and character of those crazy streets.

We ran into a couple of hookers who worked with us on a regular basis. They disclosed the lowdown on Slim and the two dudes who'd gotten checked out over at Martinez's. Apparently these guys were junk bags who did some running and heavy-duty errand work for a couple of local meth and coke dealers, one of whom was Eddie Gomez. The girls had no idea about any older man with a scar on his face or ear.

Before we left, the young streetwalkers threw us a free invitation for a quick midday release, putting Sean and me into a whirlwind of laughter.

"Thank you, ladies, but I don't think my fiancée would like that too much," I said.

"What she don't know won't hurt her, honey." The taller of the two girls, a bleach blonde and very busty, raised up her skirt, revealing that she wasn't wearing underwear.

My eyebrows shot up. "Holy shit."

Sean whacked the roof like a jockey. "Come on. Let's get the hell outta here."

We left the hookers behind and headed off to try to interview any family or friends our three John Does had left behind, including Slim's mother, who the hookers had said was about as friendly as a pit bull on a bad acid trip.

~~~

Sean and I pulled up to the eight-unit brick tenement where Slim's mother supposedly lived. We let ourselves in through the wide-open rear door, which was missing its deadbolt assembly and most of its dulled-out black paint, and climbed the stairs on the parking lot side. The carpet in the narrow hallway we turned down looked blue along the edges of the dusty baseboard trim, but it bled into a deeper shade of gray as it hit the black and muddled middle where the everyday traffic came and went.

Sean knocked on the door that had a 7 above the peephole.

"Who is it?" a voice behind the door asked.

"Providence Police, ma'am," I said. "Please open the door."

"What the hell do you want?"

"It's about your son, Slim," Sean said as he fiddled with loose change in his pocket.

I turned sideways, bracing myself, as the door opened slowly inward.

"His name's Brice, and he don't live here." She couldn't have weighed more than a buck, soaking wet, but she snarled at us with a look that could have stopped a bull in his path of victory. Her eyes were yellowed, and she was missing half her teeth.

Peeking past her, I could see where Slim had gotten his cleaning skills. Her apartment was neck and neck with her son's dump.

I could tell that no matter how we approached her, it wasn't going to be peaches and cream. I settled for blunt. "Your son was murdered last night."

"That deserter, he ain't no son of mine. Now leave me alone. Don't bother me again." She slammed the door in our face.

We stood there looking at the 7 on her door again, but this time it was like a big middle finger pointing right at us.

"Whatever," Sean said. "We have about an hour left before we have to head back. Come on."

~~~

More than an hour passed by as we combed the tight grid that lay between Elmwood and Broad. The gas hog's needle sat on empty. We were running on fumes. We had no leads and were no further ahead than when we had started.

We dropped off the GT and headed back to the station, where we started picking our way in and around the database, looking for any matches to Martinez's description of this older man with a heavy facial scar. Most of the cases that would land on my desk were either idiots acting off immediate impulse or people who were just total fuck-ups. That made most of these crimes traceable and very short-lived. This time, I had a funny feeling that we were going to be working overtime trying to sniff out a killer who probably changed his shoes around every other corner.

After two hours of staring at a screen full of degenerates and junk bags, my eyes were crossed. They burned and had started to water. "I think I'm going screwy, Sean."

Sean's eyes looked like two fried eggs that had been left on the flattop a little too long. "Me too, man. I'm tired of looking at this screen. Come on, I'll give you a ride home." He grabbed his coat off the corner of the desk and threw it on.

The fluorescent lights flickered off the shiny waxed floor as we made our way to the back stairwell, where we ran into Major Sullivan.

"How'd you guys make out today?" he asked.

I heaved a sigh. "We got absolutely nothing, Major."

"I have a feeling this guy's gonna be a bitch," Sullivan said.

"Oh yeah," I said. "I had that feeling when I jumped out of my car onto the sidewalk this morning."

"Persistence, Detectives, persistence. I'll see you tomorrow."

"See ya, Major," Sean said.

I gave him a wave, and we left the station out the back door. Walking across the back lot, I thought about the 365, 24-7 commitment we have as cops. I'm telling you, not one day goes by without some kind of bullshit.

Two patrolmen were dragging a woman across the lot who was fighting with everything she had and calling them names that even I hadn't heard.

"Years ago, they would've just slapped her," I said.

"Yeah, maybe," Sean said. "Or hauled her ass over to the mental ward."

On the way to my house, we caught a double shot of Hendrix on the radio. I watched my side-view mirror closely for any possible tails while thoughts of crosstown traffic filled up my head.

Sean squinted and looked in the rearview mirror, trying to see what I was looking at. "Why do you keep looking in the mirror? Is someone tailing us?"

"I don't know," I said. "I just don't want to take any chances. Who knows what this maniac saw today or what he has planned."

"I don't know, man. Why would we be involved in any of this?"

"You're probably right. I'm sure I'm overreacting, but you know I'm a little nuts, so fuck it."

Sean whipped into my driveway, threw the car in reverse, and put his hand on my headrest. "Just a little nuts," he replied with a smile. "I'll have a couple of patrolmen drop off your car. I have some shit to do first thing in the morning, and won't be able to pick you up."

"Okay, thanks. Just have them leave the keys in it."

"What are you doing tonight?"

"Megan came home today."

Sean shook his head with a big smile. "Oh, I see."

I whacked him with the back of my hand. "Don't think about it, you dirty bastard."

"I'm just busting your balls." Sean looked at me with a big smirk.

I opened my door and put one foot on the ground. "What about you?"

"I think one of the channels has a Rodney Dangerfield marathon going on."

"*Caddyshack*," I said. "Maybe *Back to School*."

"*Easy Money*."

"Oh my God, Joe Pesci at the bar . . . 'You know who I am?' 'No.' 'I'm the guy that put the bathrooms in this place.' 'No wonder it smells like shit in here.'"

We started laughing.

"Pesci flips out the best," Sean said. "I need something funny after this fucked-up day."

"I hear ya. See you tomorrow." I got out and shut the door, and watched as Sean backed up and drove away into the darkness.

I turned around and looked at the bedroom window, where I saw Megan waving at me. I walked toward the front door and stepped up on the big chunk of granite that was our front, and only, step. The door pulled open before I had time to twist the doorknob.

Megan stood in the doorway, with her arms open and waiting. Seeing her made me think of the first time we had met. This heavy feeling of nostalgia mixed with raw passion came over me and brought me back to our first date, when I had picked her up at her apartment over on Williams Street. Maybe I had just really missed her, or maybe it was the soul mate thing we had going on. Whatever it was, I was hungry for her body to wrap up into mine.

She was wearing one of my white tank tops along with teal underwear that was basically just some strings put together. I stepped through the doorway and onto the gleaming oak floor that Jack just had refinished. I grabbed Megan and flipped the door shut with my foot. I picked her up and held onto her butt cheeks as she wrapped her legs around my waist. She reached behind me and twisted the deadbolt shut, and then pulled off my tie. I carried her down the hall and into the bedroom, where I lay her down on the cool white sheets. She worked her way down the buttons on my shirt as I ran my hands tight along her rib cage and hooked my thumbs onto her panties, pulling them down her gleaming legs.

The heat and explosive blood flow turned me into a wild animal. I shredded the tank top in half and exposed the rest of her perfect body. At that point I was well-done and ready to go, and couldn't get my clothes off fast enough. I struggled with my tangled left pant leg, which was caught on my foot. I finally got my dress slacks free and flung them across the room and onto the bureau. I pushed down on her inner thighs and lay into her. Her soft blond hair was cool to the touch as I ran my fingers through it. It smelled like sweet fruit.

Thirty minutes and three orgasms later, we were shoulder to shoulder, totally naked, staring at the ceiling.

Megan rolled over, got up, and slipped her panties on. "Maybe I should go away more often," she said as she stood in front of me, holding her hips.

I grabbed her wrist and pulled her back into bed and under the covers for another session.

~~~

After dinner, I sat on the couch and turned on the television. "Hey, Meg, you wanna watch a movie?"

She walked into the room with a big blue storage container, placed it at my feet, and fell backward onto the couch, right next to me. "Sure, what do you wanna watch?"

I sat up and grabbed the plastic tote. The lid read *Elliot '95*. "What's this?"

"Your mother dropped it off today. She said she'd been cleaning out the attic and came across some of your stuff."

I held up my football jersey, which reeked of mothballs. It took me right back to the high school locker room. "We actually went to the championship my senior year."

"Ooh, Frantallo, number twenty-four. I definitely would've been all over you back then." Megan stared into my eyes, slightly embarrassing me.

I picked through the tote that held a chunk of my childhood between its two handles. Even my cleats were in there, curled up like bananas. "I can't imagine trying to fit into this uniform now."

Megan ran her hand across the name on the jersey I had draped over my knee. "Did you guys win the game?"

I got up off the couch and tossed my jersey to Megan. "I'll tell you, but I'm going to do it play by play, like a commentator. Okay?"

She folded her legs and sat on them, getting comfortable, and grabbed her glass of wine from the side table. "Okay, tell me the story."

I swung my arms around, warming up to give her a play-by-play description of the biggest game in Smithfield football history. "It's 1995, and it's the championship football game between neighboring towns, Smithfield and Johnston. The bleachers are packed and overflowing with fans. People are spread all around the field, grabbing onto the fence and shaking it with excitement as they root for their teams.

"We are three points behind Johnston with less than a minute to go in the fourth quarter. The teams break out of their huddles and set up post across from each other. The players dig into the abused field with their spikes, ready to collide, as the Smithfield QB, Tim Collins, sounds off with his cadence. The center, Big Chucky Pizzarro, snaps the ball to Collins at the thirty-five. Tim Collins, the heartbeat of the Smithfield Sentinels, gets into position and looks downfield to his right. Johnston has been playing great defense, fierce coverage, and flat-out pure hustle all night." I held my hands out with excitement and looked to Megan for an expression. "So what do you think so far? Do you like it?"

"Of course I do! Keep going." Megan waved me on while she took a sip of her wine.

"Okay, so the Smithfield frontline struggles, trying to hold back Johnston from ending this game. Collins can see his wall collapsing right in front of him, with time running out, and fast." I stood like a statue on the area rug, underneath the ceiling fan that was spinning on high speed, with my right arm cocked back.

Megan put down her glass. "What are you doing? Quit stopping right in the middle of the exciting parts." She threw her arms up for me to continue.

"Okay, okay, I just wanna make sure you're paying attention." I hopped back into character to finish the rest of the story. "So where was I? Oh yeah. Collins scans to his left and notices a green jersey cutting across the ten-yard line. It's Frantallo, and he's wide open. Without hesitation, he fires a rocket downfield and into Frantallo's hands. The wide receiver sees three purple jerseys coming at him full speed, intent on crushing him, and tucks the ball tight into his gut. He carves a hard left toward the end zone and dives through the air at the goal line, jumping right over one of the three defensemen. The other two pummel Frantallo in midair, and gravity forces them all to come crashing down.

"The end result is a pile of half the varsity football players on the field, with me on the bottom." I grabbed my beer and sat back down next to Megan. "The refs come charging over, their whistles blowing intermittently as they cut their way through the crowd to find out who won this game. The entire stadium comes to a screeching halt as the refs dig their way closer to who will be leaving tonight as champions.

"The fans' anticipation hovers over the field with biting concern as the clock ticks with nine seconds to go. Smithfield stands on the sidelines in the cold, frigid air, hoping there's a touchdown in their future. The refs finally get to the bottom. They peel off the last purple jersey, exposing a green one that reads Frantallo. At that moment, everyone finds out that he has full possession of the ball and is over the goal line. Both refs stand up and signal a touchdown."

Meg shrieked and clapped with a huge smile on her face.

"The news triggers full-blown excitement and craziness throughout the home-field stands. Smithfield wins their first championship since 1983. Coach Moore reaches up to the sky, dropping his folder on the ground. The field gets flooded with spectators and tons of classmates ranging from freshman to seniors. Even a couple of Marine Corps recruiters cheer along with the crowd. In fact, it was those two marines who approached me in the parking lot later on that night and got me thinking about joining the Corps."

Megan wrapped her arms around me. "I can't believe you won the game! You never told me you were a football hero for your school."

"Collins was the real hero. It was all about the throw."

"You're always so modest, babe. But that's one of the things I love about you."

We sat back to watch a movie and woke up some time later, twisted together like a pretzel, to the DVD's intro repeating itself every ten seconds. I looked at my watch, which read ten past two, and then at

Megan, who had drool running across her cheek. I woke her up by combing her hair with my hand and turned my neck left to right, cracking it, which gave Megan goose bumps.

"Oh my God, babe, that sounds sick."

We walked to the bathroom, holding our backs as if we were eighty.

Megan leaned on the door as she brushed her teeth. "What time is it?"

"Two o'clock. We have to stop falling asleep on that couch. My back feels broken."

We crawled into bed, said good night by tapping each other's hands, and passed out.

~~~

We clear out of the kitchen. I look around and see a lot of materials—boxes, suitcases, old clothing, and papers—thrown around in total chaos. It's as if a tornado ripped through here. This house smells so bad, like shit. Jeffries loses it and starts yakking in the corner of the kitchen, where a lamp stands all by itself.

"Go ahead, Elliot. I'll be right there." Jeffries blows lunch again.

I can hear the guys busting his balls as I round the corner with a smirk on my face. I leave the room because I can hear something at the end of the dark, endless hallway. I slide down the hallway with my rifle pulled up tight into my shoulder, not knowing what to expect at the end. The farther I move down the hall, the darker it gets, as I inch away from any natural light. The hair on the back of my neck stands up straight like a dog ready to get into a front-yard beef.

I flip the light on that's mounted to my rifle and approach the upcoming corner. I hear something again. "United States Marine Corps!" I yell out as I shift around the corner, quickly following my rifle's lead.

A woman, roughly sixty years old, is sitting on the floor. My light shines in her face while I ask her what she is doing in this house. I tell her to get up as I motion to her with the barrel of my rifle. She raises her arms up slowly in the air and then leans forward, as if she's bowing toward me. I feel this warm suction of air across my face. My entire body is tossed against the wall like a rag doll, and I fall to the floor, unable to see anything.

The next thing I know, I'm covered in debris. My ears are ringing, and my eyes are confused by blindness caused by cement and plaster dust that has taken over the entire house. I can't see a foot in front of me. The pulsating tone in my ears is holding control of me. That fucking bitch must have triggered a bomb when she got up.

Everything is dark and blurry. I get picked up and carried out of the house, and thrown into one of the Humvees. I open my eyes, but they burn and water, cutting my vision in half. I see buildings and this shit pile they call a country pass by me like a flash as I lie upside down.

Our medic, Chaps, yells to me over and over, "HOLD ON, FRANTALLO!" He pushes on my leg with tremendous force.

I feel my eyes roll into the back of my head, and Chaps fades away from me as if I'm sinking to the bottom of the ocean and he's watching me drown from above. I hear birds singing as I fall away into another time and place, and see them flying around me . . .

~~~

I jumped up, fully energized, and leaned over to shut off the alarm. The singing birds helped me swing into my morning and away from my nightmares a little more smoothly. The alarm was Megan's idea. She came home with it one day, which I'd had no problem with, because the old alarm clock had sounded like a garbage truck backing up in the bed.

The strong aroma of bacon and eggs floated into the bedroom, giving me a kick in the ass to get up and get going.

Chapter 5

After breakfast and knocking off some morning duties, I said my good-byes to various parts of Megan's face, neck, and body. I grabbed the rent check off the fridge on my way out, not wanting to take advantage of Jack's complacent behavior.

I walked past my car and saw Jack enjoying his morning routine. Just like a dog scratching at the door to take his morning shit, Jack was on his porch, sipping away on his double espresso and reading the morning paper. I walked up the stairs and placed the check on the table in front of him.

"What happened yesterday with the four dead guys?" he asked.

"We really don't know too much. But my guess, there's a professional out there, and if you want my opinion, the department's gonna have its hands full on this one."

Jack took a sip from his Italian brew. "It says here in the paper that it was a drug deal gone bad. Sounds like another one of the chief's bullshit cover-up stories."

"You know what it is. We can't put that kind of burden on the people's backs. The general public will freak out if they think a talented, unstable, psychopathic wild man is lurking around in their backyard."

Jack lowered his brow with curiosity. "What makes you think he's talented?"

"He's a trained sniper and a very skilled killer." I checked my watch. "Shit, Jack, I gotta go. I'll fill you in later on what I find out today." I ran down the stairs and sped off, knowing I'd have to break a few traffic laws to get to work on time.

~~~

When I pulled into the parking lot at the station, it seemed more jammed up than usual, so I parked on the sidewalk. I walked a direct path to Jimmy's office, eager to see if he had any leads for me to sniff out.

Mario, one of the maintenance men, was mopping the floor outside Jimmy's office. "Good morning, Detective Frantallo."

"Hey, Mario. What happened?"

"One of the urinals upstairs backed up and came through the ceiling.

Now I have to change the ceiling tiles, too. Man, it never ends around this place."

"Yeah, no kidding. Believe me, it ain't any better on this side." I tapped Mario on the shoulder and peeked into Jimmy's office.

"I knew you'd be down here," Jimmy announced. "I just didn't think it'd be this early."

I stepped into his arena of paperwork and disarray. "I know I'm an impatient bastard, but I was kind of hoping you'd have just one piece of something for me to go on." I rubbed my coarse, two-day scruff, anxious to get out on the paths and out of this station.

"Most of the factual evidence I found yesterday is not going to get us anywhere. The DNA results obviously are not ready yet, but we still have a shot at finding something with the autopsy." Jimmy flipped through the piles of paperwork scattered all over his desk.

I didn't want to stress Jimmy out any more than he already was. "Just keep me posted, Jimmy."

"Will do. Hey, wait a minute. Is today the twelfth or the thirteenth?"

I looked at my phone, unable to give him a solid answer off the top of my head. "Uh, let me see . . . The thirteenth."

Jimmy put his head back into his paperwork. "Thanks, man."

"No problem. Have fun." I waved to Jimmy as he flipped me off, and passed Mario, who was still mopping away. "See ya later."

"Okay, 'bye, Elliot."

I walked to my office and had just sat down at my desk when a text from Sean vibrated my beltline, asking me to take a ride. I sent him a message that I'd meet him in the back lot, at my car. I got up, grabbed my coat, and headed out to find Sean.

"We have to go back to Slim's apartment," he said as I approached.

"Why, what's up?"

"Because his mother got caught breaking in through the kitchen window. Freddy Baxter was doing a routine drive-by and caught her climbing in. He's holding her until we get there."

"You've gotta be kidding me," I said, rolling my eyes. "You know what? Good. Fuck her. Maybe we'll get a little more outta her than yesterday."

~~~

We pulled up to Victor Martinez's three-decker and saw the patrol cruiser parked out front, so we parked around back, trying to stay out of sight. The back door was wide open.

"Being here makes me think of Martinez, and how he chain-smoked about five cigarettes in under ten minutes," I said.

Sean chuckled. "Yeah, no shit."

I looked at the neighboring houses and up to the angled rooftops in the tree line on our walk across the lawn. Sean and I let ourselves in to see what this woman's story was, and to find out why she couldn't wait another week to get into her son's apartment.

Patrolman Fred Baxter stood in the corner, biting his lip, with a look on his face as if he wanted to backhand this scumbag. Slim's mother, who sat on her son's clothes-covered couch, looked at us as if she wanted to say, "Oh, here we go again."

"Ma'am, I'm Detective Kelley, and this is Detective Frantallo," Sean said. "We were at your apartment yesterday. We're very sorry for your loss, but you cannot be in here, let alone take police evidence." Sean waved his arms around in a very soft manner, trying to be as cordial as possible and not blow his top.

"I told you yesterday, I don't wanna fuckin' talk to you," she hissed. "Now, all this shit was my son's. So now it's mine, okay? So back off before I get a lawyer, yo." Slim's mother conveyed her talk-show attitude, pivoting her head side to side and throwing around outlandish hand gestures at the three of us.

She really was just adding gasoline to a fire, because at that point, we were ankle-deep in bullshit and tired of hearing her mouth.

I lashed out at her, starved for patience. "Listen, lady, you obviously don't know the law, or what you're even talking about. So unless you want to get arrested for obstruction, trespassing, breaking and entering, tampering with a crime scene, and about ten more things I could slap you with, you'd better get the fuck out of here."

"Get her the hell out of here," Sean directed to Baxter.

Baxter was happy to see her go. He wore a smile as he walked her out the door to the sidewalk and shut the gate behind them.

"Imagine her!" Sean exclaimed. "Yesterday, that piece of shit disowned her own blood. She wouldn't answer one question, and then she slammed the door in our face."

We looked out at her hanging out at the curb, continuing to go off and acting like a complete jerk.

"She's probably over here looking for a quick fix that Slim might've left behind," I said.

"Probably. Or maybe to scrape up some of this coin." Sean waved his hand and pointed at an anthill of change on the glass end table next to the couch.

Sean checked out the bedroom, climbing in over the dirty laundry, frozen pizza boxes, and Diet Coke cans that were scattered everywhere.

I sifted through the pile of change and noticed a couple of crinkled-up receipts. I pulled them out, exposing a couple of roaches and some ribbed Trojans.

I checked out the receipt that had first caught my eye. "Here we go, Sean."

"What'd you find?"

"This receipt." I held up the crumpled paper. "It's from a car rental place over on Broadway."

"We could definitely go over there. Maybe they know him."

"Take a look at the date," I said.

Sean grabbed the stub and took another look. "Son of a bitch. I think we need to see what they know over at Jake's Rental Palace."

We headed out and locked the doors of the empty tenement.

~~~

"It looks like they're out of business," I said as we rolled up to Jake's. "Check out the sign on the door."

Sean and I pulled into the small lot, but it was full of cars.

"Fuck it," I said. "I'm gonna block the driveway."

We got out of the car and headed into the main office, where two men were staffing the front desk.

"Can I help you, sir?" the younger of the two asked.

"Sure, help us with this." I placed the receipt faceup on the counter in front of him.

The older man picked up the receipt and looked it over. "We can't help you with that, man."

"Is there a manager around we could talk to?" I asked.

"Sure, man," the older guy said. "Paul, go get Lance."

Paul left to retrieve his boss from the back.

The Big Cheese came out from a little office in the rear of the showroom and approached us, wiping a napkin across his mouth as he finished chewing whatever he'd been working on when Paul had interrupted him. He stood just a few inches over five feet and had a full head of tight brown curls.

Lance looked up at Sean and me with a big smile. "How can I help you guys?"

I pushed the receipt forward. "We need some info on this."

He placed both hands on the counter. "Well, guys, there's nothing I can do, here."

We revealed our badges to the boss man. "We really need to know about this particular situation."

He hesitated, looked at the receipt again, and then looked at us. "I'm not supposed to give that kind of info out to anyone. It's corporate policy."

"Look," Sean said, "this is involving a murder investigation, and it's very serious. So give it up now, here, or we'll have to take all of you downtown to give it up there. It's your choice."

"C'mon, man," Lance whined. "We're going to the Sox game this afternoon. We're supposed to be leaving in an hour. We don't have time for that." Nervous that we were going to fuck up his plans of footlongs and draft beer, the manager pleaded that we not bring them in.

I pushed the receipt another inch closer to falling off his side of the glass countertop.

"All right, listen," he relented. "I'll tell you what I know."

The two salesmen stared at the situation like sheep staring at the side of a barn.

"Four guys came in yesterday." Lance sang like a bird, not wanting us to jam a stick in his spokes.

"What did they look like?" Sean asked.

"Um . . . The black guy was like a toothpick. Five ten, six feet, I don't know. Oh yeah, he had a Raiders coat on. Oh, and he had a chipped tooth on top." Lance, trying his best, went through the motions with us, using gestures and body language to help us out and get us out of his hair. "The other two guys were Spanish, both of them around six feet tall, too." He held his hand up over his head, sizing up the heights of our suspects.

"One of them had a tattoo on his hand, like a snake or something," the older salesman said. "I remember because the mooch cleaned out my candy bowl. I friggin' hate that." He picked up the empty bowl, clearly pissed off.

"What about the fourth guy?" I asked.

"He stayed outside," Lance said. "He was much older than the boys who came in."

"How old?" I pried at him, feeling that we were freeing something up.

"I'd say late sixties."

"Yeah, and a real cagey bastard," Paul said. "He never once looked in here." The younger boy to our right pulled up his pants and pointed outside to the front lot.

Lance continued. "These three wise guys were in here bragging, saying that their boy outside was hooking them up, and that after they finished some job, he was taking them on vacation to Florida."

"Let me guess," I said. "They paid with cash?"

Lance nodded his head. "Yup."

I looked around at the surveillance system. Cameras were in every corner of the office and lobby area. "Do the cameras work?" I asked, pointing to one above the door.

"Of course."

"Can we take a look?"

"Be my guest, Detectives." The boss man waved Sean and me around the counter and invited us into his office.

We followed him, and the smell of Italian grinder smacked me in the face as I crossed over the threshold into the twelve-by-twelve area that gave Jimmy's mess a run for the money.

Lance set the DVR for the correct time to see the thugs, Slim, and our mystery perp. The half-eaten grinder, sitting on Lance's desk in its white oil-stained paper, was making my mouth water. I looked at my watch, which revealed only that I never ate on a normal schedule. Papers, invoices, and stacks of pamphlets sat around his desk like a series of mountains up in the North Country.

"Look, there he is," Lance said.

We all looked at the guy on the black-and-white screen. He kept his back to the camera the whole time, just like the young salesman had told us.

"What kind of car did they take?" Sean asked.

"They didn't take anything. They were supposed to pick it up today and drive down to Florida. It's the blue Honda CRV out front, waxed and ready to go."

Sean and I looked at each other. Neither one of us knew what the hell was going on.

My phone started to ring, and a familiar number displayed across the screen. It was a sergeant I'd gone through the academy with. I excused myself and answered the call. "What's going on, Phil?"

Phil spoke into the phone as if there was a gun to his head. "Megan's been shot, Elliot."

"*What!*" My heart started to pound.

Sean turned to me, knowing something was very wrong.

This phone call was about to make me go upside down, fucking bananas. "Talk to me, Phil! What happened?"

He started to lay out the details, then cut himself short. "We have a lock on 'em. Head to I-95. They'll most likely hop on the interstate and make a run for it. I gotta go, Elliot." Phil ended the call abruptly.

I stood in shock for a few seconds to get my head right. "Come on," I said to Sean. "We gotta go right fuckin' now!"

I pushed open the double doors, and we left the showroom and the salesman behind. I flew out to the car with Sean tailing right behind me, trying to keep up. I blew through the parking lot like a hurricane.

"Hurry up, Sean! Get in the fucking car!" I turned the key in the ignition, starting the engine, and slapped it into drive. I cut the wheel quickly to the left with the palm of my hand and punched it.

Smoke poured off the rear tires as the unmarked cooked the rubber off them and slid sideways, leaving a 180 in the middle of the road and across the double yellow line. All traffic ceased as I swerved down the road with the lights on and my foot buried into the gas pedal. I headed east toward the city, with intentions of intercepting the subjects of the fucked-up phone call I'd just received.

My switch had flipped and turned me into a fucking lunatic. I drove that unmarked Crown Vic as if it was a Formula One car. I hopped onto the sidewalk to pass the cars that were in my way in front of Classical High School, while Sean held on for dear life.

"Elliot, what the hell happened?"

"These guys hit the bank where Megan works. They shot the place up and hit three people. One of them is Megan."

"You gotta be kidding me!" Sean picked up the radio and held it close to his ear. "Patrol has the car in their sights. They're declaring there's a driver and two assholes who are armed and dangerous."

I drove off the sidewalk, hopping the curb at better than eighty. As we approached the west side of the interstate, I squealed around the corner and looked across the highway at the eastbound ramps that headed north.

"There they are." Sean pointed across the freeway, spotting the criminal chase that we were about to join.

The three assholes hit the ramp, leaving the Allen's Avenue area, and hopped onto the highway. They cut into traffic, causing mayhem immediately. There were a few cruisers on their tail and more heading toward the on-ramp, trying to stay with them. I grabbed a pack of chewing gum I kept in the ashtray and popped a piece into my mouth.

"Elliot, I can't believe this is happening right now," Sean said.

"I swear to God, Sean, if I get my hands on these pricks, they're all dead." I pushed the cruiser to its limit and stayed close to the chase from above the interstate, heading for the next on-ramp. "I'm going to kill these motherfuckers!" I howled, gripping the wheel as adrenaline flowed through my entire body like a bad disease. I pulled on the wheel, wanting to snap it off the column. The veins in my neck were solid and beet red. "What is it, Sunday? Move! Get the fuck out of the way!" I fought through the dead wood that was slowing me down with fury and conviction and finally made it to the overpass, where the on-ramp to I-95 was going to put me in the chase. "Look at this goddamned traffic!" I smashed the dashboard with frustration.

"Fuck it, Elliot. Go around 'em." Sean whipped his hand across the front seat with everything he had and pointed to the left.

I drove down the wrong side of the road and directly toward oncoming motorists as we cruised by all the bumper-to-bumper traffic that was entering the city. Sean sat up, keeping tabs on what was going on down below on the interstate, while my brain sank deeper and deeper into the confusion and instinct of cold-blooded murder, and my own special talents that turned me on.

"Hold on, Sean!" I cut the wheel, slid around the corner, and got onto the ramp as the cruiser's ass end drifted across the pavement.

Sean gripped the door, bracing himself as the tires broke free and whipped us back straight and on target toward the interstate. I hugged the inside corners and bossed my way through the heavy congestion, kicking up dirt and debris that had collected on the shoulder over time.

"Holy shit, Elliot, look out!" Sean gripped the seat and pushed his feet against the fire wall as we squeezed between a bright white SUV and the Jersey barrier. He looked over at the speedometer. The needle read a buck thirty and was continuing to climb. "I didn't think this piece of shit could go this fast."

I kept my eyes focused on the road, and on the chase that was just ahead. As a marine, you're trained that when someone in your unit gets hit, you don't become passive, you become aggressive—you attack. I'd actually kind of missed that adrenaline high.

Sean and I passed the marked cruisers that were chasing these maggots as if they were standing still. The target was about a hundred yards ahead of us, so I let off the gas, not wanting to pass them. The guy in the backseat of the white Buick shot out the window and kicked it onto the trunk. The busted-up back window fell from the trunk onto the road, and we ran right over it. Then the asshole in the backseat started unloading on us with an AK. Bullets bounced all over the hood, hit the windshield, and flew right by us.

The shooter pulled the rifle back into the car to change clips, which gave me an open window to punch it and attempt a pit maneuver. The driver read my mind and stood on his brakes, catching me off guard and causing the hood of my car to nearly go under the ass end of the Buick.

"Holy shit!" I yelled and cut the wheel hard, which threw us off course and into an unsteady sideways squeal. I counter-steered, cutting the wheel back, and lost control. The unmarked skidded violently across three lanes of traffic as I stood on the brake. The other two cruisers lost total control and drove right off the highway, trying to avoid an almost monster collision.

Sean looked at the two marked units that were down the embankment and out of commission. "Holy shit. That was fucked."

We pulled over as the dust cloud cleared and exposed the cruisers.

"Are you guys okay?" Sean yelled out the window.

"Go, go!" Paul Rinard screamed up, leaning against the hood of his cruiser and pointing up the highway. "Let's get those assholes."

I nailed the gas and made my way back to the left lane, looking for the strategic driver who had vanished into thin air. "They had to have jumped off the next exit."

Sean and I looked down the pin-straight highway, with no visual of the suspects in sight. I kept the pedal cranked down and got to the next exit as fast as the car could get us there. We went barrel-assing down the ramp, skidding sideways, and came to an abrupt stop at the light. I looked down Branch Avenue to the right. It was full of traffic.

"Elliot, look! The car, it's right over there." Sean grabbed the radio and called in the quick discovery.

I punched it, disrupting traffic once again, and bolted over to the empty lot, amped up and ready for whatever was next. We rolled up on the white Buick parked at the end of the lot. Its front bumper had been pushed right through the chain-link fence.

"Car looks empty," I said.

Sean shook his head. "The bastards must've gotten away through that hole over there."

I looked over at a missing section of the tall fence that abutted a big abandoned brick mill and Route 146. We got out to check the car and approached the vehicle from either side with our guns drawn. It had appeared that the getaway car was empty, until I walked up to the front passenger side and looked in. The guy who had been in the back with the AK was still there and still holding his rifle, but he was slouched over, and his brain matter was splattered all over the backseat like an art collage.

Sean glanced into the rear driver's side window. "What is this shit?"

"I have no fucking clue." I was getting more and more puzzled the more we looked into whatever it was that we were involved in. I peeked in the front seat. "Oh, nice. Wait till you see this."

The copilot lay across the console with his head in the driver's seat. Blood was pooling on the seat cushion, leaking from a stab wound to his right ear. I saw a bag on the floor beside his right leg, which had been bent back at the knee. I opened the front passenger door and grabbed the bag, and opened it to find with little surprise that it was full of money.

"Same fucking MO as Wood Street," I said.

Sean leaned in through the driver's window. "Elliot, what the fuck is going on? What's this guy's deal? What, is he a serial killer that doesn't like money? Or maybe he's just a vigilante with a conscience."

"Or maybe he just doesn't give two shits about anything but taking these pricks out," I responded, my mind and body deflating from the high-speed ride. "I gotta get the fuck out of here and find Megan. What hospital did they take her to?"

"She's at Rhode Island. Take the car. I'll catch a ride with one of the guys."

"Thanks, Sean. I'll call ya later."

I jumped into my car and hopped back on the highway. I sped back the same way we had just come, southbound toward the city. I looked across the highway to see a couple of flatbeds pulling the two cruisers out of the ditch.

~~~

I picked up my phone as I neared the hospital, and dialed Phil. "Phil, talk to me. How's she doing?"

"I'm just leaving the hospital now. She's in somewhat stable condition and going into surgery, but her coworkers both died."

"What exactly is wrong with her?"

"The bullet is lodged in the top of her left lung. She's unconscious." Phil related the news to me with some difficulty, choking on his words.

"Thanks for staying with her." I held it together as I thanked Phil, but when I hung up the phone, I started to shake with anger.

I pulled into the fire lane, got out of the car, and sprinted toward the main entrance of the hospital. The oscillating glass entrance spit me out into the lobby, and I moved rapidly to the front desk to find out where Megan was located.

The receptionist made solid eye contact with me. "Can I help you, sir?"

"Yeah, hi, can you please tell me where I can find Megan Brown? She came here by emergency rescue."

The woman punched a few keys. "She doesn't have an assigned room."

"No, she was just rushed in with a gunshot wound."

"Wait a minute. Is that the poor girl who was involved in the bank robbery?"

"Yes, she's my fiancée."

"I'm so sorry, honey. She just went into surgery. Cut across through the main glass corridor and into the east wing, past the gift shop."

"Thanks for your help," I said, already walking away.

I started to make my way toward the ER. The mass confusion in the main lobby was like beach traffic on Route 4 in August.

I pushed my way as politely as possible into the waiting area that sat outside the ER, trying to find Megan, who was fighting for her life. "Excuse me, could you please tell me where Megan Brown is? She was shot in the bank robbery."

The short, five-foot brunette nurse, wearing pink scrubs and holding a box of orange juice in her hand, pointed me to the OR right across the hall. "I'm pretty sure they're operating on Megan as we speak."

I waited outside the OR, getting up from my seat to pace about every fifteen minutes, hoping for someone to come and give me a bite on what was happening.

The door swung open, and a tall doctor in his late forties approached me.

I jumped up. "Doc, I've been staring at that door for the last hour and a half."

A look of doubt washed over his face, telling me the news was not good. "Hi. I'm Dr. Bentley."

"Elliot Frantallo," I said and shook his hand. "What's going on here, Doc?"

"Well, first of all, Megan's surgery was a success. But she is unconscious, and may stay that way for . . . well, I really don't know how long."

"Is she going to pull through, Doc? Will she live?"

"I believe she will. But she has suffered some serious lung and tissue damage. It's probably better, in a way, that she's out of it. This way, she won't move around, which could aggravate the wound and cause more substantial damage. This downtime might just allow her body to do the healing it needs." Dr. Bentley explained the procedure and all possible outcomes in a somber tone.

"How long . . . How long before . . . before we know if she's gonna wake up?"

"That I can't tell you, my friend. That's up to her, or someone else bigger than her—or me or you." The surgeon shook my hand with a look on his face that said, *I really don't know what to tell you, man.* He turned around and pushed back through the same doors he'd come out of.

The door clicked closed, and then reopened within seconds. A nurse came out and introduced herself to me. "Hi, my name's Krista. I'll be taking care of Megan as long as I'm in the building."

"Thank you, nurse. Please take care of her as if she was your sister." The whole fiasco had finally hit me, and I wiped at the tears that began to flood out of my eyes and down my face.

"Please, call me Krista. And I will. You have my word. Listen, why don't you go to the cafeteria and grab a drink or something to eat while we get her room ready. Give us a couple hours to put it all together, and then come up to 312. That'll be her room number."

"Okay, thanks a lot, Krista. I appreciate that."

~~~

I took her advice and headed for a quick bite and a large iced coffee. I kept Sean in the loop via texts while I walked through the lower levels of the hospital. It was industrial and conditioned with a certain cadence that made me think of boot camp and my time spent in the Corps. I stepped off the shiny waxed floor and onto the rear service elevator, along with a janitor who was holding a fluorescent lightbulb as if he was waiting on deck in the big leagues.

"How are you doing today?" I asked, nodding his way as we started to move.

"I'm doing okay. Same shit every day." The middle-aged janitor shrugged his shoulders and chuckled.

"Hey, did you know Victor Martinez, by any chance?"

"Sure, he was my boss. I mean, I guess you could say he was my friend, too." A look of sadness came across his face, and he dropped his eyes to the floor.

"I'm sorry for your loss, umm . . . I'm sorry, I didn't get your name."

The young, balding janitor stood next to me in dark gray coveralls that were two sizes too big, with tall cuffs sitting on top of his curled-up, shiny black boots that pointed to the sky. "Oh, sorry, my name's Thomas." He reached out to shake my hand.

I exposed my badge and shook his hand. "Was Martinez ever in any type of trouble with anyone that you know of?"

"No way, man. He helped everyone. One day he just showed up at my old apartment to help me move into my new house. I never even asked him, you know? He just knew I was moving and wanted to help. That was Martinez."

"Sounds like he was a good guy." I grabbed the stainless handrail as the elevator slowed down from our short ride.

Thomas put his hand out and asked if that was my floor. I stood in a fog of puzzle pieces that swirled around me, making it hard to see straight.

He held the elevator door open with his leg and asked me again. "Sir, is this your floor?"

I focused my eyes to his voice and apologized. "Sorry, I'm just feeling a little out of sorts." I walked out of the elevator and leaned against the wall, trying to catch my bearings. I didn't know what was going on.

"Are you okay?" he asked.

"I'll be fine, thanks, Thomas."

He gave me a concerned wave and pointed me to the room directory on the wall across from the elevator as the door shut.

I took a left and then a quick right, following the plates at every opening, before I walked into the room that was marked *312*. Megan lay silent and peaceful, right next to the heartbeat of the floor, the nurses' station. I regained complete focus, watching her lie there, lifeless, with tubes and lines all over her.

A nurse popped her head in the room, startling me. "Are you her husband?" she asked, a bit on the overprotective side. Her eyes were reading me—I hate to say it, but—the way a cop would.

"Not yet," I answered, "but I will be." I flashed my badge, trying to ease down her guard-dog instincts.

"Oh, okay. I'm sorry to come off a little rough, but with the circumstances at hand, we all agreed to keep a close eye on her."

"Please, don't apologize. I want you guys to watch everything and trust no one."

"The police told us they had already informed you. I take it you're Elliot?"

"Yes, ma'am."

"We contacted her sister, whose number we got from the bank. She's on her way."

"That's great. I didn't know how I was going to make that call." I held onto Megan's hand, wondering how in the hell this could have happened. "Please tell me she's going to be okay."

The nurse patted me on the shoulder. "Your fiancée has been through a lot, but she's a tough cookie, and that's what she'll need to stay alive."

I heard the footsteps of someone entering the room at a good clip. I looked up and saw Krista.

"We're running tests and will be monitoring her vitals closely for the next twenty-four hours," she explained. She walked around the other side of the bed and checked Megan's pulse and IV drip.

Megan's sister, Denise, walked into the room not ten seconds later and broke down immediately, dropping her pocketbook on the floor. She collapsed on me and emotionally lost it. "I can't believe this, Elliot. How could this happen? My sister's never hurt anyone. Why did this happen? Why her?" Oversized tears fell from her eyes, born of the devastation that had hit both of us right across the face that day.

The two nurses calmed her down with hugs and reassuring words.

"I don't know, Denise." I said. "I just don't know anything anymore." I wanted to tell her the whole city was fucking crazy, but I kept my mouth shut, knowing that she'd been against Megan moving there with me in the first place.

"I'm going to stay with her, Elliot." Denise explained that she had taken time off from work and was not going back until Megan returned home. "Go do what you have to do to find the bastard who hurt my baby sister. I'll call you with any updates." She wiped her eyes with conviction and hugged me tight.

Chapter 6

I pulled up near the station and parked the unmarked across the street from the entrance. I wanted to check in with Jimmy and see if he had any new leads. I walked across the street and looked up the road to the abandoned building that sat north of the station, a sad and lonely two-family tenement with a storefront on the bottom level. Roughly four years ago, the second-floor tenant had fallen asleep with a lit cigarette and burned the place up like a barbecue.

I noticed an older man leaning against the building at the corner of Dean and Carpenter, smoking a butt. He was wearing a cap and kind of fit the description that Martinez had spilled to us. The man was too far away for me to grab a valid ID, so I changed direction and upped my pace from a stroll to a steady power walk.

I moved up the sidewalk, digging into the new concrete footpath that was no more than a year old. "Excuse me, sir. Can I ask you a question?"

The man turned his back and disappeared around the corner, totally ignoring my request. I pulled out my sidearm and started booking my ass off toward him, but rounded the corner with caution. I was surprised to see no one but a couple of kids bouncing a basketball.

I didn't want to waste my time or energy running around the neighborhood, chasing an obviously very sly fox, so I walked back to the path I'd briefly stepped from and made my way back to the station.

~~~

I knocked on Jimmy's door as I opened it and poked my head into his office.

"Hey, Elliot," he said, looking up at me. "What's wrong? You look like you've seen a ghost."

I shrugged. "I'm okay, Jimmy."

"I've been waiting for you. Nothing too earth-shattering, but the knife wound is definitely interesting. Something strong for us to go on."

That got my attention. It was our first and only lead. "Where did the weapon come from?"

"Definitely government issue. I was actually able to hunt down three like matches, but that's as far as I can go. I can't narrow it down past that, because the same blade is used on all three knives. Only the handles change, depending upon what branch of the government you're in."

"So how do we find out what military branch issued the knife to our guy?"

"The battalions don't issue them. The CIA does." Jimmy sighed and looked at me, disclosing his thoughts of trouble for anyone close to this case.

"I knew it right away, that day he popped Martinez. I could feel a dominating presence lingering in the streets. It had spook written all over it." I wondered if that had been our guy next door, flirting with the department to see what and how much we knew.

"Oh, and not to change the subject, but the crystal meth in the bag at Martinez's is the same shit associated with that big bust that happened in July." Jimmy slid over the file he had grabbed from vice on that particular bust that somehow Eddie Gomez had weaseled his way out of and pinned on Joel Ferguson, his competition.

"No shit . . . Do we have any idea who the bank robbers are?" I squeezed my fist, wishing I could have killed them myself.

"Yeah, their names are . . ." Jimmy dug out a file from underneath another one and flipped through it. "Here it is. David Reese and Trip Howard. These two mutts have a book full of arrests. Here, check it out." He handed me the file.

I opened up the manila envelope. "Unreal. Possession with intent to distribute, burglary, rape, aggravated assault, arms charges . . . These jerks have been at it since they could walk." I tossed the file onto the table, sickened by the two scumbags. "These pricks should've been in prison."

"A twenty-two behind the ear is cheaper."

"Yeah, no shit. Any paperwork on the knife?"

"Actually, yes. I do have pictures of the weapon printed up." Jimmy rustled through the piles on his desk once again. "Here we go, right here." He dropped a couple of color printouts on the tabletop in front of me, and a folder fell onto the floor, spilling its contents everywhere.

"What the fuck?" I picked up the papers and looked at the knife that was breaking all the records.

I'd seen similar knives, but not quite the same. It was long, sleek, and intimidating. The handle was what really looked different from other knives I'd seen like it: solid black, with a checked pattern that came to a point on both front and back, and a bronze seal of an eagle in the middle.

With Megan flooding my thoughts, I gave the papers back to Jimmy and decided that tomorrow was another day. "This is definitely a good start, Jimmy. I'll talk to you in the morning." I put my coat on and took off, closing out the day.

~~~

My drive back to the ranch took fifteen minutes longer than usual. I drove around, using the city streets, trying to shake any tail I could have possibly picked up on my trip home. After pulling into the driveway, I parked behind Jack's car and shut off the ignition. I grabbed the steering wheel and squeezed it, staring at the speedometer I'd almost buried earlier today. I stepped out onto the slight decline of the driveway and shut my door. Jack stood at the end of his porch, waiting for his daily report, totally unaware of the devastating news that I was about to unload on him.

"What's wrong?" He looked into my eyes, which recited a short story to him.

"I'm okay."

"Bullshit, you are. Come on and tell me what's wrong."

Jack was an expert at reading people's feelings. He had told me that most people wore them on their sleeve or pinned to their lapel.

"It's Meg, Jack. She's been shot." Numbness passed through my chest, choking me, and the words had to fight their way out of my mouth.

"*What!* What the fuck are you talking about?" Jack, shocked with the knuckleball I had just thrown his way, bellowed out a cry of anger and whipped his beer bottle against the side of my apartment, breaking it into a million pieces. Shards of glass rained over the driveway and onto our cars. "Come up here." He waved me up to sit down and hang out, and then he disappeared inside.

I really wanted to go home, but I knew that talking with Jack would keep my mind off the negative feelings that I'd otherwise only obsess about. I sat down at the table on his porch about the same time he swung open the door and placed a bowl of pasta and beans and two fresh beers on the tabletop in front of me.

"Eat, kid. You have to stay strong. Now, tell me what the fuck you're talking about. How the hell did this happen?"

"Two scumbags robbed Megan's bank today and shot the place up. They hit her and two of her coworkers."

Jack took a swig of beer, holding his waist with his left hand. He walked to the street side of the porch and leaned against the bannister. "What's her status?"

I lowered my eyes. "She's in a coma, Jack."

Jack spit onto the curb below, and everything went quiet. Even the breeze passing through the porch spindles added to the awkwardness of the moment. Jack rested his forearms on the railing, staring at the street and sidewalk below. I forced myself to finish the meal he had given me, even though my appetite was nonexistent.

Jack turned around. His demeanor had changed from when we had started this conversation. "Who the fuck are these assholes? Do you have any leads on them?" He paced side to side, with a fire in his eyes that seemed to call for lanterns and pitchforks.

"Yeah," I said. "They're actually at the city morgue, getting ready for a dirt nap."

Jack's plans of revenge were instantly flushed down the toilet. "So you guys dusted them already?"

"We didn't, but we're pretty positive the sniper, or vigilante, or whatever he is, wiped them right off the fucking map." I wiped my mouth and put my napkin in the empty bowl.

"Really? What makes you think that?"

"Well, there are a couple things. First of all, both crimes had money left behind, and let me say that both times it was a pretty substantial amount. Yesterday's bag had over fifty thousand bucks' worth of crystal meth in it, and today's score was the bank's bag of money, once again left behind in the front seat of the getaway car. Please, tell me, who would leave something like that behind after going through all that trouble? And on both counts, like it's a hobby for this guy or something. Second thing, both murders involved a stab wound in the ear." I tipped back the last of my beer.

Jack stopped dead in his tracks while opening up the screen door. "Excuse me, what did you say?" He stood in the doorway, frozen.

"What?"

Jack looked at me with a steely glare that held me down and commanded my full attention. "Did you say a stab wound to the ear?"

"Yes. Three victims yesterday and one today had a knife slid into their ear and bottomed out in their melons."

The screen door shut behind Jack as he walked inside. I watched him through the window as he slowly stepped across the living room floor. He seemed deep in thought, on a personal excursion in his mind. He followed the same footsteps on the way back. Then he sat down and slung a beer across the table into my hand.

"What's wrong, Jack?" I asked, wondering if the wound he was licking was going to bring the night to an abrupt end or get it rolling with a war story about how he had gotten it.

Jack wiped the top of his beer can with his sweatshirt. "I never thought he'd come back."

"Do you know this guy?"

"I do. I followed that motherfucker back in the early seventies." Jack sat back and opened his beer. "*Salud.*" He held up his cold can, clunked it into mine, and took a long swig.

"Is he military?"

"He definitely has deep military roots that came from somewhere. His father, maybe. Or someone else in his family who was ex-military. He was way too creative and powerfully dangerous for a young guy, Vietnam or not. He had to have been brought up through the ranks as a kid." Jack shook some peanuts into his hand and popped them into his mouth.

"Were you ever able to pull a file on him? Get a name? Anything at all?"

"This guy was very squirrelly, and not easy to get close to. Somewhere in his life he got fucked up bad. He had this intuition that always kept him a step ahead of everyone, even me. Depending on what his personal experiences were—a bad childhood, abuse, possibly depression—Vietnam would've been the last shovel of shit that tipped over the wheelbarrow on this guy."

"What happened?" I asked, wondering how this guy had slipped through Jack's iron claw. "Why did you stop looking?"

"I never stopped looking, kid! Every time I went on a call, I always wondered if his trademark would appear and possibly lead me to his trail where I could pick up on his scent again. In '72, my partner, Billy Reardon, and I were on a stakeout unrelated to the vigilante, or whatever he is. We were perched in this sweet hideout that was out of everyone's sight. We had a bird's-eye view of a lot of shit that we turned our eyes away from because we were on his trail exclusively."

"Did you ever see him from that spot you guys had?"

"Oh yeah. We saw this guy who fit his description, but we weren't a hundred percent sure. This guy basically put Billy's wife into a mental meltdown for the rest of her life."

"What happened to his wife?"

Jack paused for a moment, biting the end of a cigar. He lit it up until it glowed a hot amber. "We'd been following this other douche, Sunny Martello, before the whole thing with Billy's wife. He'd been brought for questioning and was being held until we were certain of his innocence. Billy and I knew we had to get back to the station to question that asshole Sunny, but we had this other guy in our sights at the hideout." Jack drew off his short, dark cigar, letting the thick, dense smoke pour out of his mouth and into the heavy night air. "Our man was sporting a heavier beard than the five-o'clock shadow he'd been wearing at our last and only visual we'd had up to that point. That made us reluctant to jump on his back immediately.

"We watched him as he walked into this abandoned building right next to our post. Billy wanted this guy in a bad way because of what had happened to his wife, Brenda, but that's a whole different story. That poor thing worked over at the hospital off North Main Street as a nurse. Great job. They had actually just bought a house and were ready to start a family. They were starting a little late in life, but I have to say, they were madly and truly in love." Jack stared off for a moment. He pulled another thick drag from his cigar and puffed away, lost in his nostalgia. "I don't know what I'm saying. I'm getting off topic here.

"Brenda was on her cigarette break when she witnessed a colleague of hers get stabbed to death by this madman. She watched him insert a knife and bury it into the victim's ear. It sent her into a downward-spiraling nightmare. After that, forget it. She drove Billy crazy with her fear and insecurity."

"That sucks."

Jack wiggled the tab off the top of his beer can and popped it into the half-full mason jar where we'd been collecting them. "Oh, it sucked bad!"

"I'm really sorry this is bringing up so many bad memories for you."

"Brenda was never the same after that, and in a way, neither was Billy. Within a year, she moved out, and Billy wasn't too far behind. He had to leave the city. He quit the department to save his marriage, and her. So they sold me the house." Jack started to laugh, and bit the cigar with his teeth.

"What is it?"

"Before Billy left, he fucked a couple of guys up real bad. Sunny Martello got it the worst. He just got caught up at the wrong place, wrong time. Billy was walking the double yellow line every day, and really didn't give a shit anymore. He lost his mind and became extremely volatile. He actually left at a good time, because the department was on him like flies on shit. But I have to say, Billy and I had some great times." Jack looked at his smoke, thinking back to those memorable moments with his good friend.

"So who did this madman kill at the hospital?"

"A janitor. Lester Johnson was his name. He'd been selling morphine out the back door to a local dealer. We'd known about it for a few months, but wanted to catch him in the act with something worth more than a slap on the wrist or some simple probation bullshit the judge would have entertained."

"So what happened?"

"The janitor, Lester Johnson, was taking a cigarette break at the same time as Brenda, but down the Sixth Street alleyway. Brenda, who was out having a cigarette with some other nurses, heard cries for help. She left the girls to check out what was going on, but rounded the corner too late, and witnessed Lester, whom she worked with every day, being stabbed in the head. She went into shock right on the spot, and our killer vanished into thin air like a fucking ghost. No other witnesses."

"Is that the last time you heard from him?"

"No. Two weeks later, the local dealer, Tim Wells, who'd been buying the morphine off of Lester, got whacked in his living room with four of his runners. All of them were fucked up beyond bad." Jack gulped down his beer and crushed the can flat. "That crime scene, to this day, was the worst I've ever seen. It was like a hyena had been locked up, starved, and poked at with sticks through the holes in its cage, teased and taunted, making him more wild and devastating than he already was. Then some genius opened that cage and ended the game. These guys were torn apart. Some of their faces had been ripped right off their skulls."

"Holy fuck, are you serious?" I had a clear picture of the massacre in my mind. Along with my own personal experience of this guy's handiwork, Jack portrayed such a vivid description that I felt as if I was there. "I hate to sound like a broken record, but when he made that shot through the back window of my moving car, from where he was located, I knew that this killer was going to be a serious fucking problem." I finished my beer and placed it on the table next to his flattened aluminum twelve ounce. "So what happened to your partner Billy? You know, back at the stakeout?"

"I'll tell you what, let me go get a bottle of bourbon, and I'll tell you the whole story from beginning to end." Jack, mentally smoked out, walked into the house more slowly than usual, and with his head down.

I texted Denise, looking for any updates on Megan's vitals. The text came back in a flash that her condition hadn't changed. I finished up my finger conversation with her by asking her to keep me in the loop, and to pray.

Jack returned to the table with two tall shot glasses and the famous old No. 7 Tennessee favorite.

Chapter 7

After a few shots, Jack began to narrate his story to me. At that point, we were well on our way to being corned. Jack didn't hold back on any details as the story flowed out as if it had all happened yesterday.

I listened to the craziness of the old days, and watched the paintings and quick sketches from Jack's words appear before my eyes like flash cards. The story got me into a different zone. As I found myself keeping up with Jack, drinking into a lighter shade, I started to pay attention to stuff like chipping paint and toothed-in clapboard pieces that added to the character of the neighborhood. Everything became richer and clearer in the personal focus between us.

Jack hit me with each stroke of his brush as he exaggerated every vivid detail about the man he had chased. He put me in the driver's seat, as if I was reliving his dark past alongside him. Some points in his story were so raw that if a cop had done those things today, he would be the one going to prison. Don't get me wrong—I wished they would bring those days back and stop wiping everyone's dirty asses and runny noses.

Jack looked at his watch and finished the shot that had been staring at him. "I have to go get some rest, Elliot." He stood up and shook my hand.

"I'll see you tomorrow." I thanked Jack for everything and stumbled home, more than half snapped and looking up at the crystal-clear, starlit sky.

I stopped in front of the chunk of granite at my door. It was inviting and warm, and pulled me in like a magnet. I decided to accept the front step's invitation and finish the inch of Jack Daniel's that was left in the bottle. Jack turned his lights off and joined the rest of the neighborhood in total darkness, and I took my hard seat and looked down the street that would share a quiet moment with me.

That street, like many others on the East Side, revealed a lot of mystery at night. The houses were old, and I'm sure they had many secrets hidden within them. My father was a plumber, so growing up, I frequently thought about the immigrants who had moved here and built the cities that we lived in. They built what we see, and more importantly what is hidden—under the streets and in the walls, where no one cares to notice. Back in the day, all phases of construction were mostly built with manpower and common sense, but today, with all the tools and technology we have, sometimes it makes me wonder. Having no pride in the way you conduct your actions will eventually be the demise of anything worthy to your soul.

"Hey, that's what I think, at least." I talked to myself quietly as the alcohol brought about deep feelings in the night.

Even though we were in the busy city, it was very peaceful at night. That was when Megan and I would go sit out there, on that big chunk of stone, and look at all the old houses. We would make up stories about what had happened through the years in each house, and make a game of it while drinking a couple of beers. I could always remember one particular story I had made up for her, the story that had changed my life. I had picked the house with the brick front, two doors down on the right.

~~~

"The man who lived in that house was a hermit, and a bit of an introvert," I said. "He never left the property. He had everything delivered to him, even his laundry. He was living off a big inheritance that his uncle, a bootlegger from the Deep South, had left him."

Megan laughed.

I smiled back at her and took her hand. "One day, with no warning, his life changed forever. He was reading a book out on his front porch, and a beautiful woman walked by his house. She threw a smile his way and talked to him with her eyes, and invited him to do the same.

"Now, understand that this man had not stepped off his property in four and a half years of living there. Let me also tell you this man was very handsome, and many women over the years had smiled at him as they walked by. This time was different. He could not take his eyes off this beautiful woman whose physical language had laid a path for him as she walked by. She was about to disappear around the corner, and before he knew it, and with no hesitation, he found himself on Brook Street, asking her to marry him."

I asked Megan if she thought my character was crazy. She told me she thought he had a few issues. At that point, I got down on one knee and told her that a woman who could look into a man's eyes and get him to break his routine, who could peel him away from his comfort zone, from everything that he was acclimated to, should not be allowed to disappear around the corner.

"So the question stands," I said. "Is he insane for his impulsive behavior, or is he brilliant for recognizing true love when he sees it, and then acting on it? Living in the moment?"

Megan looked at me with a smile that lit up her entire face and asked me softly, "Elliot, are you the hermit in the story?"

I looked into her glossy, nervous eyes as she bit on her bottom lip with anticipation.

~~~

A couple of loud, drunk college kids walking by pulled me out of my past and reminded me that I had to go to bed. I got up, shook the sadness off my back, and sent out a text to Denise. I shut the front door behind me and climbed into bed, on top of the comforter, and passed out fully clothed, thinking of Megan, Jack's story, and the history of the city.

~~~

Jack sat down on the edge of his king-sized high-post cherry bed, wearing a white, V-neck T-shirt and light blue boxer shorts. He brushed off the double shot of Jack and placed the glass on the nightstand beside him. He looked at his hands, studying their signs of age, and thought about the endless experiences he'd been through. He lay down and groaned as he stretched his legs, tightening them up through the cold, virgin sheets.

Jack reached over and shut off the lamp that stood next to his empty glass, and stared at the same dark and light shadows that peeked through his window every single night. His eyes got heavy as his mind replayed the events of the night, and the stories he had told consumed his thoughts as he drifted off to sleep.

~~~

Jack opens his eyes to someone knocking at the front door.

Bang, bang, bang!

"Hold on!" he hollers. He pulls up and buttons his pants, and heads over to open the door. "Morning, Billy."

Billy comes walking in, chomping on an apple. "Did you forget about our recon mission today?"

Jack shuts the door and follows him into the kitchen.

Billy stands in front of him, his frame rugged and hair thick and red, picking away on his apple. "You still wanna do this, right?" He claps his hands together, full of piss and vinegar.

"Yeah, of course. Just let me finish getting dressed."

"Let's take your car in case we need the power."

Jack tightens his belt and looks over at his nightstand, and spots a set of car keys. He grabs them and follows Billy out the front door. They walk down the driveway, and Billy lifts up the garage door. Jack almost falls over. Sitting there is a 1966 AC Cobra. He can't believe there's a Cobra in his garage, and the keys are in his hand. It's a dark green color, with a 289 engine and saddle interior.

"Are you going to sit here picking your nose, or are we taking this girl out?" Billy says.

"Yeah, of course. Get in." Jack opens the driver's door and slides down in the seat.

"Good. She needs some exercise." Billy shuts the passenger door and slaps it with his hand, as if he's priming up a purebred to run the derby.

Jack fires her up and takes off down the road. The rumble from this beast, bouncing off the houses, along with the ridiculous acceleration, gives him goose bumps.

They cruise the upper East Side streets that are much cleaner and filled with loads of people walking the streets. Billy navigates them through the crowds of hippies that flood downtown and across to Federal Hill, into the Italian section of the city, where the Mafia still controls everything.

They get to their favorite location, hidden away like a bird's nest, built into the side of a cliff. It has a panoramic view of some hot spots that get heavy foot traffic of all types. They are using it to stake out a drug dealer who may be linked to the murder of a minor. Usually the Mob takes care of dirtbags like this, but this guy keeps slipping through their fingers.

"Here we go." Jack points to the abandoned building across the street, where a bearded man comes walking out. "That guy right there fits the description of the fucker who melted Brenda's brain." Jack looks down and watches him get into a big green Dodge Coronet.

They hit the back stairs at full speed. The stairs are so steep that Billy and Jack may as well be skiing down them. They hop in to the Cobra, and Jack turns the cylinders. He whacks the gas and flies up the alley between the two buildings, just wide enough for the mirrors to fit. He shoots out the alley onto Atwells Avenue without even looking. He's trying not to lose this guy.

The partners are a few cars back and can tell the bearded suspect is getting anxious. As they tail the perp, he picks up speed and starts driving erratically, which pisses Billy off.

"See, why is this asshole getting nervous? He wouldn't drive like this unless he's guilty of something. He grew a fucking beard, thinking he was going to be invisible." Billy fidgets in his seat like a kid on a candy high.

They stop at a red light, sitting five cars behind the perp. He decides red means go and lights up the tires, terrorizing the traffic in the intersection kamikaze style, almost causing a major pileup, and starts to pull away from Jack and Billy.

"Punch it!" Billy screams.

Jack dumps the clutch and puts it to the boards, frying the tires, and races between the cars on his left and the storefronts on Billy's side. He double-clutches and whacks the stick into second, blowing posi right through the intersection that is still in shock from the mayhem created by the 5,000-pound target in their sights.

The Cobra straightens out, with the intersection behind them and their daredevil villain up ahead. Jack pushes her into third, and the Cobra leaps up like a wild animal launching after its prey. The tires grab the pavement, snapping their necks back as they gain on the bench seat with wheels.

The demented madman with the lead foot is definitely past the point of a routine traffic stop. He bangs a quick left up a one-way into the jewelry district, just missing a couple of kids with the ass end of his car as he chatters across the choppy pavement sideways.

Jack decks the clutch, breaks to the fire wall, and almost passes the street as he slides the Cobra around the corner, feathering the clutch out and mashing the gas back to the boards. He counter-steers from the raw horsepower as smoke billows off the tires, while Billy gets a good look at the real estate on either side of the road. The lightweight power plant whips back and forth, shifting through second and third gears as they gain on the perp.

Up ahead, another car joins in the chaos by choosing the street that they are totally abusing, and approaches the suspect head on as he flies up the skinny one-way street. The big green boat intimidates the lightweight Chevy Nova off the road. It hobbles up over the curb and smashes through the front of a barber shop, blowing out the plate-glass window. The Coronet comes spitting out of the one-way, its tires screaming as they almost fold right off the rim. Jack slides out around the corner after him, as if he's skating on glass glued to the back of the unknown man's ass.

The cars are racing down North Main Street at better than a buck twenty when Billy decides it's time to pull out his .44. He rips it from his shoulder holster and pulls back the hammer with a big smile on his face. Billy hangs over the door and points the small cannon at the moving target, shooting off the side mirror. The second shot disappears into the trunk, leaving a hole the size of a bottle cap. The two-lane road they've been using as a drag strip is coming to an end, and fast . . .

"Billy, get in your fucking seat, now!" Jack screams as they approach the T-intersection at speeds that feel surreal. In the blink of an eye, the asshole stands on his brakes, forcing Jack to do the same. Billy pushes on the dashboard so he doesn't fly through the fucking windshield. Both cars skid around the corner at a good clip and continue to collaborate in terrorizing every vehicle they share the streets with during this historic Providence car chase.

Their guy makes a sudden demented move and gets on the interstate, traveling the wrong way. He weaves in and out of oncoming traffic that shoots at him like BBs. Against Jack's better judgment, he follows the perp and deals with the aftermath the guy leaves behind.

The man turns up the throttle and bulldozes through the congestion. He cuts left and squeezes between two cars, steel scraping violently as he presses through them. One of the cars spins out of control, and the old man driving behind the wheel heads right for Jack and Billy. Jack can see the fear in his eyes as they almost collide, but he cuts the wheel, avoiding the head-on crash, and drives up the embankment on the side of Interstate 95.

The Dodge fires up the highway, clearing his own path, as Jack concentrates on riding out the bank and trying not to flip over. The tires kick out dirt and globs of grass all over I-95 as Jack fights to find his way back onto the pavement safely, but by then it's too late. He's gone.

"What the fuck!" Billy screams. "I can't believe he's gone! Fucking prick got away again. Head back to the station, because we have some shit to take care of with our boy Sonny."

As they head back to the station, Billy doesn't say much. He chain-smokes a couple of cigarettes and stares at the blue sky through his aviator sunglasses that Jack had brought back from 'Nam and given to him.

They get back to the station, and with no hesitation, Billy starts going through the file on Sonny. Billy has about twelve years strong on Jack with the PD.

"We've been through this with this prick before." Billy looks at Jack with blood in his eyes.

A plainclothes officer walks into the room. "Hey, I thought you might want to know they're letting that scumbag Sonny Martello fly."

Billy slams his fist on the table. He picks up his coffee mug and smashes it against the side of the filing cabinet, like a full-blown lunatic. "We have to stop this motherfucker before he fucks up anybody else!"

The people around them stand there like corpses, and complete silence fills the room. Jack and Billy head down to the cells where they are holding Sonny.

Billy demands that the officer in charge of the tank get him out and bring him into the interrogation room. "Bring that prick in here."

Jack can see where this is going. He thinks this guy is about to have a very bad day. They grab a cup of coffee and sit down in the room.

"Listen, Jack," Billy says. "Today, I'm good cop, and you're bad cop."

Jack looks at him with a tad bit of confusion. "What do you want me to do?"

"Let me tell you something, kid. Whatever it takes. If this guy gets out of line, I want you to split his fuckin' head open like a ripe watermelon. You scar this motherfucker so that every time he combs his hair, he thinks of you. Do you understand what I'm telling you?"

The officer brings Sonny into the interrogation room and sits him down at the table.

"Wait outside," Billy orders. He waits until the officer leaves and closes the door behind him, and then directs his attention to Sonny. "What's going on here, Sonny? We chased your friend all over the fucking city."

Sonny, a medium-built, middle-aged wannabe gangster punk that Pasquale "Big Fingers" Nardo, Providence's crime boss, could possibly whack because of the underage allegations that are being brought against him, sits there with a stupid look on his face. "I don't know what you're talking about, cop. Now be a good boy and give me the phone!" Sonny tries to push them around with his cockiness and total disrespect.

"Why do you have to play games, Sonny?" Billy grills him again. "We saw you several times with him over next to Richie B.'s place. So tell me, why is he running?"

"I ain't sayin' nothin' without my lawyer. Give me a phone!" Sonny repeats. He gets hotter and turns a darker shade of red every time Billy pumps him at the podium.

"You know your friend with the beard? Why were you with him over on Atwells, near that board-up you guys are using for your personal sugar house?" Billy gets louder and begins to reveal a much harsher persona every time Sonny opens his trap.

"Guy with a beard? I don't know who or what the fuck . . ."

"Just answer the fucking question, you piece of shit!" Billy screams and flips one of the chairs ass over teakettle across the room and into the wall behind the cocky suspect.

"I told you before, go fuck yourself. Now give me the phone. I'm tired of repeating myself to you pigs!"

"Sonny, innocent people are . . ."

"What, are you deaf? PHONE, PHONE, GIVE ME A FUCKING PHONE, YOU ASSHOLE COP!" Sonny flips his lid and stands up, yelling and screaming at Billy with spit flying out of his mouth. He is furious and waves his arms all around, acting like a baby who isn't getting his way.

Billy looks at Jack and gives him the green light, so Jack stands up and grabs the rotary phone off the desk, pulls the cord out of the phone, then brings it down along his side. He faces Sonny, who is still going on about who knows what. Jack hears nothing but annoyance while walking up to this loudmouth. Sonny turns and looks at Jack with no regard, spraying his dribble Jack's way now as he decides to stay on the same bumpy road and continues going off on his tantrum.

Jack looks into Sonny's eyes. They are empty and without regard. Jack sees someone in front of him who doesn't care about anyone but himself. Then Sonny pushes the wrong fucking button and makes Jack's decision very easy.

"Go fuck your mom," Sonny says and spits on Jack.

That's it. *"You want the phone, you fucking cocksucker?"*

Sonny must see it in Jack's eyes, because the outburst stops. This prick telling Jack to go fuck his mother just filled the bedpan right to the top, making it impossible to carry without making a complete mess. Fury lashes out of Jack like a lightning bolt.

Jack takes the phone and smashes Sonny so hard the phone rings, making Sonny fall back and hit his chair, flip right over it, and fall flat on his back. Blood pours from his head like a volcano erupting as he lies there screaming. Jack hops on top of him, still holding onto the receiver, and wraps the cord tight around his neck. He chokes him while smashing his head over and over with the phone earpiece.

"What's wrong, asshole?" Jack needles him, as he tries to fit the receiver in Sonny's mouth and shove it down his fucking throat. *"I thought you wanted the phone."*

Sonny's eyes roll around looking for an escape from the suffocation and total domination that Jack holds over him.

"Jack, Jack, that's enough. You're gonna fucking kill him." Billy rips Jack off him.

Jack is like a wild baboon in the jungle that has just lost his mind. He looks down at Sonny, who is bleeding all over the place. It looks as if he fell all the way down a cliff on his face.

"Hey, Jack, you can play bad cop for me anytime." Billy opens the door and signals the young officer with just a facial expression.

Mike Boyle, a young cadet fresh out of the academy, walks into the room and sees Sonny lying there looking like he's been hit by a moving truck. He grabs the top of his hat as if he's in a wind storm. "Holy shit!" Mike yelps out, shocked by the mess and depredation that has filled up the ten-by-ten room. "What the fuck happened?"

Billy looks at Mike and says, "This stupid prick tripped and hit his head, trying to call his mama."

~~~

Jack opened his eyes and looked at the clock on his nightstand. It was only four in the morning. The stories he'd told Elliot ran deep in his subconscious. He rubbed his eyes and thought of the dream that would always stay with him, no matter what happened.

Chapter 8

My alarm clock woke me once again, but this time from a very vivid and sensual dream about Megan. I was so used to the routine nightmare in which I revisited my friends—and, sadly, their deaths—that I actually felt a little incomplete that morning. I really didn't know if I'd ever get over the guilt of walking away from the explosion that took my guys off the map and walking out of what had become my reality.

I stood up, pulled my hair back, and hiked up my boxers. I drew aside the sheer curtain and looked out my bedroom window to see if Jack was on schedule. To my surprise, he wasn't there. He must have swapped out our cars and gotten off to an early start. I let the curtain go and buzzed through the house. It felt totally empty. It needed Megan's . . . everything.

As I drove to work, I looked at the city, and thoughts about Jack's story rolled around in my head. The sharp similarities between the perp I was actively becoming obsessed with and Jack's early '70s villain were uncanny.

I stopped by the hospital to check on Megan, but nothing had changed. I held her hand and whispered in her ear, hoping she could hear what I was saying and would fight her way back to me.

Denise, sleeping in a god-awful twisted position on the cream-yellow-and-white flower-print commercial sofa, woke up. "She's gonna pull through, Elliot." Denise pulled her hair back and sat up, yawning, her right hand covering her mouth.

"I know she is. I know she can hear me. I can feel it, sis."

"Have you found out anything about who did this to her?"

"A few things, but nothing concrete."

Between the pain in Brenda's eyes and Megan lying there all busted up, with monitors beeping, tubes running all over her, and a pale tone to her skin that was three shades lighter than normal, I was finding it hard to keep positive and play the role I was accustomed to.

I leaned over and kissed her forehead. "Keep me in the loop, big sis."

Denise got up and gave me a hug. I turned and left the two sisters in room 312, along with a piece of myself.

~~~

Road work around the station put a damper on the parking situation, so I pulled into the visitors' lot. It was packed and giving me anxiety as I tried to maneuver around.

"Fuck it," I voiced to myself. I threw it in reverse, backed out of the lot, and pulled up onto the curb. I parked on the grass, facing the abandoned house I had run over to the day before.

I looked at the board-up, wondering if our perp used shitholes like it as his camouflage. In Jack's story from the previous night, the suspect had entered and left an abandoned building.

The house had the words NO COPPER INSIDE—ALL GONE spray-painted on the faded blue vinyl siding. I really wanted to go check it out, but I didn't think smashing down the doors was going to be a smart move against a player of his caliber. Instead, I got out of my car and walked into the station, never once turning and looking at the abandoned dump that sat two hundred feet from the nose of my car. I knew that if I wanted to hop on this guy's wavelength, I'd have to play his game of patience and strategy.

I entered the west side of the building and passed by the polished granite wall of recognition, where decades of brother officers stared at me while I walked past them. I passed the elevator, but then stopped. My intuition was telling me to head up to the top floor and find my way onto the roof.

I hopped into the stairwell, climbed the four flights, and ran around looking for the scuttle. I found it in the janitor's closet, and stared at the matte-finished maroon steel ladder that led straight to the roof. I pushed open the two-foot-square hatch and climbed onto the rubber roof, staying concealed below the parapet. I made my way past the rooftop unit that sat near the northwest scupper and faced the abandoned tenement.

Lying on my stomach out on the edge brought back memories of being in charge, and being ready to end someone's life with just a quick pull of the trigger. Martinez's house popped into my mind, making me realize that I should go back and recon the quadruple homicide from higher ground. I stayed low and dropped down the scuttle door, pulling it shut behind me.

I immediately called Jimmy and asked him to look into Vietnam snipers who had come out of the Rhode Island area. I thought that the list was probably a short one, but it was worth a shot. I ended the call and dialed up a buddy on SWAT. I asked him to meet me in the locker room with a scoped rifle.

On my way to the locker room, I swung by my desk and checked for any new messages. After listening to a bunch of long-winded crap, I looked at the time and headed to meet Jake, my sniper buddy, who'd been on SWAT for ten years.

I was sitting on a bench in the locker room, answering some earlier texts, when Jake came in and leaned the case on the locker next to mine.

"Model 700?" I asked Jake as I stood up and locked hands with him.

"Oh yeah. I put a couple of boxes of ammo in there with it, just in case." Jake tapped the case of the long-range weapon.

"You know I'll take good care of her," I said.

"If anyone asks, you didn't get it from me."

"I broke in and stole it." I smiled. "C'mon, you know me better than that."

Jake chuckled. "I know. I just get nervous."

"How are the wife and kids, Jake?"

"They're fine, man. The real question is, how's Megan?"

"She's fighting."

"I want you to know, if you need anything at all, my family and I are always here for you."

A few words, a quick handshake, and a hug sent me out of the barracks and back on the trail that I was actively hunting day and night.

~~~

I wasted no time grabbing my unmarked and driving to the opposite side of the building, out of sight, to load the obvious case into the trunk. I hopped onto the highway and once again grabbed three digits on the speedometer.

I wanted to make it to Martinez's without being seen, so I switched out cars at impound. I hopped into the quiet cruiser and headed back to Martinez's in my hooded-out ride.

I pulled up to the three-tenement where all this shit had started. I drove around back and parked under an old grapevine. Sunlight poked through some spaces in the vine, making different shapes and shades on the hood of the car. I got out and looked around, popped the hatch, and grabbed the case, and then I shut the glass and walked away as if it was any other day.

I let myself in through the back door, which still had a lockbox on the handle. The glass in the old varnished door rattled as I pushed it shut. I stood on the bottom landing, listening to the house in total silence, and caught a whiff of death still coming up from the basement.

After standing still like a statue and breathing through my nose for at least a minute, I climbed up to the third floor, where Martinez had lived. When I got to the brown-painted landing outside his apartment, I noticed another door that was closed with a bolt through the hasp to keep it shut.

I pushed the door in, taking pressure off the hasp, and pulled the bolt out. The old six-panel door was buried under probably twenty coats of paint, and its hinges squealed as I swung it open. The paint on the opposite side of the door was old and cracked, and it matched the cream-colored stairs and surrounding woodwork that led up to what I guessed was the attic. Touches of light blue and teal were visible through the splits and chips that had been pulled off over many years by curious and fidgeting fingers.

I reached the top step and had to bend down so I wouldn't whack my head. The heat of the clear and open attic was intense. I saw some old soda boxes full of empty bottles, along with an oak-framed mirror that sat atop a bureau or some type of dresser. My skin started to itch with sweat, and I could feel it beading at the top of my forehead. I wanted to get the hell out of there before I needed a change of clothes.

I walked over to the window dormer that faced the west side, where Martinez's bullet had come from. I kept my distance from the window as I looked out at my unlimited options, determined to follow through with my plan.

I placed the rifle case on the floor and opened it. I grabbed the Remington Model 700 heavy barrel, equipped with a ten-by-fifty-mil dot scope, and took it in my hands to get a good feel for the piece. I flipped down the bipod and lay with the rifle on the floor, positioning myself at an angle to stay about two feet back from the window, and scanned through the houses in the area where I thought the shot had come from. I got a clear eye on a faded green house with boarded-up windows, just like the house next to the station.

The window in the attic was uncovered, except for a sheet hanging in it. I moved down the house, looking through the scope, but could only see the top floor. The rooflines of the other houses were blocking my view.

Being behind the rifle took me back to Camp Pendleton, California— to sniper training, and to some pretty hairy classified missions. I needed to get into this guy's head, so I pulled up the sash on the window and got acquainted with my rifle.

I did some quick math and transferred my calculations to the scope. I rested my finger on the trigger guard and took one last breath with the crosshairs on my target: a shingle at the right corner of the dormer on the green house, level with the middle of the window.

I knew the frame of the building could structurally handle the impact of a bullet, so I squeezed off the shot and checked to see where it had hit. The shot was perfectly on the corner, but about a foot too low. I dialed in the scope, made the proper adjustments, and readied to take another shot. I pulled back the trigger and made my second shot, which hit within a couple of inches. I was doped in close enough and didn't want to draw too much attention to myself, so I thought it was time I went to visit this dump I'd just used for target practice.

I had just put the rifle back in its case when I heard someone come in the back door and start walking up the stairs. I looked out the back window and saw an unmarked next to the shitbox Mustang I'd driven there.

"Elliot, where are you?" Sean hollered to me up the back hallway.

"I'm up here, in the attic."

"It must suck carrying groceries up here!" Sean complained on the homestretch to the third-floor landing. When he finally made it up to the attic, Sean gave a quick glance at what it was that I was doing in a dead man's attic. His eyes grew two sizes when he looked at the all-black .308. "What the fuck are you doing with that?"

"Sean, listen. I know you're going to think I'm crazy, but I have to do this my way. If we go by the rule book page by page on this, we're definitely going to come up empty-handed."

Sean held his forehead and peeked at me through his fingers. "I don't know, man. You could get in big trouble."

"I don't ask you for much, bud. If it wasn't Megan in that hospital bed right now . . . Look, just turn your head for me this one time, and I promise, if it all turns bad, I'll be the one standing knee-deep in shit. You can dump the whole goddamn pile right on me."

Sean sighed. Then he put his head down and scratched the hairline on the back of his neck. "I know you're going to do it anyway, so fill me in, because I haven't been knee-deep in shit in a long time, and I'm tired of smelling so good."

I didn't want to drag Sean into the middle of my speculation and see him get fucked because of my guesswork. But I also knew that arguing with my Irish consort would be like arguing with an Italian about food. So I saved my breath, and the valuable time that we had, and invited him to come with me to check out my recent objective.

We navigated our way back down the narrow stairs and hopped in the Mustang, still trying to maintain an undercover position to keep us from the eyes that may have been watching from afar. Sean got an earful on the ride over to the house that I'd been checking out from the attic, about my suspicions and the things that had drawn me there.

We pulled up to the three-decker that stood tall in the middle of the vinyl-sided jungle and parked on the side street. We sat behind the car's smoked-out windows like a couple of shrubs in the dark, talking about possibilities and where to look next. I looked over Sean's shoulder and saw something that grabbed my attention.

I interrupted our conversation, mesmerized by what I had just noticed. "I can't believe it." I asked Sean to roll down his window.

Right there, in plain view, was a giant billboard spray-painted on the old, faded green asbestos siding. It read NO COPPER—ALL GONE in the same orange color as the house next to the station.

"Sean, do me a favor. I'm gonna go check this place out. See if someone down at the tax collector's office can tell you who owns this house, and if they own any others in the city—the one next to the station in particular."

Sean got on the horn right away, and I grabbed a baseball cap out of the backseat. I pulled it on tight and stepped out of the car.

I shut the driver's door and walked around the back of the house, looking for an obvious entrance, or for something else to reach out to me. I passed through the fence, which had no gate, and into the backyard, where a two-car garage was rotting away with a blue vinyl tarp nailed to the roof. It had ripped and was draping down before the overhead doors. Everything looked quiet and undisturbed, so I walked up to the back door. I knew it was locked, but I checked it anyway.

I wanted to kick the fucking door right in, but once again, I had to keep it under control and ultimately keep the PD from riding my back. So I walked back down the steps and around the side of the house, where the shared driveway divided the property from the identical shithole next to it that stood tall and wrapped in vinyl. The siding on the neighboring house was damaged from cars rubbing up against the jet out, since the houses were so close.

I looked at the dirt lot in the back and saw a parked Buick Riviera with fancy wheels and a big-money paint job. I heard a knock on the window and looked up immediately to catch a couple of guys yelling at me and then bolting away from the window, disappearing.

In no time, the aluminum front door crashed open, and they were strutting up the driveway toward me. They approached me, talking shit and pointing at me.

The bigger of the two guys was repeatedly punching on his hand. "What the fuck you doing? This private property, asshole!"

"Listen, guys, I'm from the insurance company. I'm here doing a safety audit on this place, so go back in your house and mind your own business, okay?" I spoke in a serious tone and with an extreme level of confidence to the two nose bags who stood in front of me.

The guy on the left, who was a solid 200 pounds, clapped his hands below his waist. "Hey, what, do you think you're funny, bitch?"

The smaller of the two degenerates spouted off, getting in my space. "I think we should fuck this boy up, Rob. Whatchu think?" Then he threw a cheap sucker shot my way.

I read his body language and moved to my left, avoiding the sucker shot, and hit him on the bridge of the nose with a tight overhand ridge chop, knocking him back. Then I followed up with a side kick to the top of his knee and dropped him to the ground.

The big, lanky six-foot-plus, who had some gang ink on his arms and a gold tooth that stared at me from the middle of his snarl, took advantage of my blind spot and hit me in the side of the head. The head shot, although not solid, knocked me back and opened me up. He tackled me on the ground, and we rolled around on the bumpy driveway. Rocks and broken pieces of asphalt stabbed me in the back as he lay on top of me. I wrapped him up with my legs, making it a little tougher for him to move.

As we continued to wrestle around, I saw his friend get up. He was a little dazed, but I was sure he was still pissed off enough to kick me while I was tied up by the gorilla. I couldn't take that chance. I had to change the odds and call on my friend, which was going to be too bad for them.

When I graduated from the academy, Jack had given me one of his original blackjacks that he'd carried. I reached up, took it out of my ankle band, and cocked my arm back. With a quick flip of the wrist, I whacked the prick right in the mouth as hard as I could.

"Ahhh!" he cried out. "You son of a bitch!" The struggling on his end stopped without delay, and he rolled off me.

I got up to see him holding his mouth, blood leaking through his fingers. I looked at my other opponent, who was now back on his feet and standing tall.

"I'm gonna fuck you up, boy!" He charged me like a bull, with an ugly hay baler for a punch.

I blocked his arm and smashed him in the nose with a quick sweep once across the mouth. The big punk went down like a ton of bricks and joined his buddy, who would probably have to eat his meals through a straw for a while. I noticed some teeth on the ground, along with a lot of blood.

I heard knocking on the window and looked up to see an old lady in a flowered housecoat, probably their grandmother, holding a phone to her ear and yelling "911" at me as she shook her fist.

I ran across the backyard to the other side of the house, not wanting any publicity, and jumped in with Sean. I slapped it in first and dumped the clutch to get the hell out of Dodge.

"What the fuck happened?" he asked.

Two cruisers screamed by us, heading to the address. They were going to need an ambulance.

"Two assholes tried pounding on me in the driveway." I wiped blood from my brow and observed the cruiser convention in the rearview mirror.

"Were they in the house? Do you think one of them is our guy?" Sean grilled me, trying to weld together bits and pieces so he could make sense of the pandemonium.

"No, these guys came from the next house over. I think they were just looking for a fight." I pushed in the clutch and coasted back into the dimness under the vine, staying out of sight while I dropped Sean off at his car.

We made plans to put together a crime board back at the station. An ambulance blazed by, and its siren not only chopped up our conversation, but also deafened us for the moment. Then we watched another cruiser fly by.

"It's just a matter of time before someone sees us and starts asking questions," Sean said.

"I think you're right. Let's get outta here."

"What the fuck, man! I don't know how I let you talk me into this shit." Sean slammed the door shut and sprinted to his ride.

I watched him slide into his car while I crawled in reverse out from underneath the grapevine. I eased out the clutch to idle by him and saw his face light up. He rolled his window down and signaled me with his index finger to do the same.

"I forgot to tell you," he said. "I talked to Sheila over at the tax collector's office, and the house we just came from is owned by a properties company that also owns a hundred and sixty-five more properties around the city, including the one next to the station. This properties company is huge. Sheila was familiar with the outfit and told me they own property from here to Florida, along with shopping malls and restaurants. Oh, and that's not all. I also talked to Jimmy Taylor. You were right. It was a three-thirty-eight bullet that killed Martinez."

I glared at him in the side mirror as I watched him pull away, and then I did the same, leaving all of the confusion behind.

Chapter 9

I swung home and pulled up in front of Jack's house, rubbing the blackwalls of the unmarked cruiser against the antique granite curbing.

He looked down from the front porch, where he was eating a sandwich and sipping on a beer. "Come on up, Elliot."

I shut off the ignition and walked up the porch steps.

"Sit down," he said, patting the seat of the chair next to him. "I have half of a prosciutto and provolone with your name on it."

"You eat it, Jack." I grabbed a good look at the sandwich and realized my stomach was empty.

"Come on, it has the peppers my cousin Toni makes. Sit down and take a load off." Jack tapped his fingers on the table, insisting that I eat.

Between the homemade peppers and the fresh meat from up on the Hill, I couldn't resist. "Okay, you twisted my arm." I could never turn away from Jack's hospitality, so I sat down and dug in as if I hadn't eaten in a week.

"Yeah, sure I did," he said, wearing a big smirk.

"I have to talk to you about this vigilante," I said with my mouth full of food.

"First things first, kid. Tell me how the sandwich is." He pointed to the oversized grinder that he had put a lot of love into.

"Do you even have to ask? You know it's my favorite. No one makes pickled peppers like you and Toni."

"Okay, that's settled. What do you wanna know?"

"This guy in your story."

"What about him?"

"Well, you mentioned that you and Billy either followed this guy or happened to trip over him coming in and out of abandoned houses. Did you see him around these board-ups a lot?" I picked at his brain like a bird pecking on a chunk of suet, hunting for any knowledge or leads that Jack might have had locked away in his memory.

"I don't think so. Actually, I think that building in the story was owned by Nardo himself." Jack looked at me with a curiosity that ran through the wrinkles in his forehead. "Why, do you think there's something special about these board-ups?"

"Yeah, I kinda do." I washed my dry mouth down with a glass of water Jack had put in front of me along with the grinder. "I was actually thinking these houses might just put us on the right path."

"Kid, you gotta go on your instinct, like I always tell you." Jack looked at the sun and sneezed.

"*Salud*," I told Jack as he wiped his nose.

"Thank you."

"Let me tell you, this morning I thought my hunch was a little premature, because all I had was a guy who fit our perp's description smoking a butt outside the house next to the station. But when I looked out Victor Martinez's attic window and saw a thin sheet hanging there in the window of an old house nearby, it tickled my curiosity. So I drove over to the house. It's abandoned, and it has been clearly marked that the copper has been robbed, and with the same orange color of spray paint as the place next to the station."

"Well, it sounds to me like you have a big lead folded up in your back pocket." Jack lit a cigar, filling up the area with smoke. "I don't mean to change the subject, Elliot, but how did you get the gash?" He pointed his big fingers, along with the stogie, at my head.

"A couple of douche-bags needed to get inducted into the mind-your-own-fucking-business club," I answered and ran my fingertips across the egg on my head. It was still sore.

Jack bellowed out a laugh that came straight from his gut. "Did they meet my best friend, Black Jack?" He looked down at my ankle while chuckling with the cigar between his teeth.

I laughed along with him. "You know they did."

Jack loved that shit. He'd wake up and come alive when he talked about splitting heads. He'd get the same way when he talked about his time in 'Nam, serving with the Air Cavalry, and all the crazy shit he'd lived through and survived.

"Jack, listen. You know the board-up next to headquarters, right?"

"Yeah, of course. Old man Morris used to live there. I can remember when he had the penny candy counter downstairs." Jack explained how he used to buy a small bag of candy and walk the beat when he first got on with Providence.

"Yeah, well, that place, where I saw that guy yesterday who fits our perp's description, and the house where the sniper took post and pecked out the back of Martinez's head in my backseat, are owned by the same company."

"Now that's very interesting, Elliot." Jack leaned back in his chair.

All of a sudden, my radio in the car started to blow up. I bounced down the stairs, grabbed the talker off my front seat, and asked dispatch to repeat. I turned down the volume and held it to my ear.

"Holy shit!" I yelled out. "There's been an explosion off Westminster Street. A fucking three-decker got leveled. I'm sorry to chew and screw, Jack, but I have to go." I turned around to see Jack already walking down the porch steps to my car. "Where are you going?" I asked, confused.

"I'm coming with you." He climbed in the passenger's seat of the cruiser and shut the door.

I wasn't going to argue with him, to be honest. Maybe Jack would be able to shine some more light on this shit show.

I jumped in and ducked down a few streets and hopped on the highway to save time. I couldn't fucking believe how much crazy shit had gone on in the past few days. As we approached the area, I began to smell the smoke and the smoldering remnants of whatever was in the house.

We rounded the corner onto the street of the residence that by then was just a smoke signal. I squeezed through all the fire and emergency vehicles that were staggered all over the place, attending to the disaster they had on their hands. I put the car in park and got out.

Sean greeted me somewhere around the driver's side front fender, eager to start crawling through the secrets of 65 Briar Street. "The neighbors around here are saying the house was a possible meth lab, but we have no priors for this address. We'll see if the boys dig up any leads on meth ingredients." The passenger door opened, turning Sean's head. "Hey, Jack. What's going on? I didn't even see you." Sean walked around the hood and greeted Jack with a handshake.

"How's your old man?" Jack asked with respect.

"The same as always—typical mick! Guy's got a head like a cement mixer, and he's more stubborn than ever!"

"Yeah, I know. Me and your father go way back. We busted a lot of fucking heads back in the day. Your dad is one tough motherfucker. He had my back more than once. You make sure to tell him I was asking for him."

"Will do, Jack."

Sean's father, who had about ten years on Jack, had retired at the twenty-year mark to take another job as the head of security at a precious metals plant over the line in Massachusetts. He'd told us some crazy stories about the old Providence and about young Jack.

The three of us walked over to the foundation where the house once stood. We looked at the disaster that had spread throughout the area and affected the other homes that bordered the property. I discreetly scanned the area, looking for a board-up or anything suspicious in sight, with our guy in mind as the number one suspect.

Everything in the immediate area had been renovated or was in the process. Maybe it actually was just a regular day in the city, and these morons were just too high on the shit they were making.

"Over here!" one of the firemen yelled out with the excitement of a fresh find.

We walked around the right side of the foundation to get a closer look.

"What is it?" I asked Hal, the lieutenant on Providence Fire who'd called us over.

Hal looked up to respond to me and saw his old buddy. "Hey, Jack!" he yelled up, happy to see an old legend.

"Hey, Hal," Jack responded with a smile and a wink.

"Well, guys, we have three bodies right here. It looks like they were huddled together, and then all hell broke loose and tumbled down on top of them." He pulled up on a box spring that had covered the dead bodies like a blanket.

"Does it look like a lab explosion?" Sean inquired.

"I'll tell you what. Look right here. There's enough ingredients to fill a fucking dump truck. I think you could supply your whole neighborhood with cold meds for a year." Hal picked through numerous name brands of cold and flu pills, acetone, liquid drain cleaner, and other under-the-kitchen-sink chemicals.

Jimmy called to us from the southeast corner of the building. "Guys, come over here."

We rapidly moved across and over all the debris to see what the new discovery was.

Jimmy squinted, not yet recognizing the ride-along apprenticing with me. "Jack, how the hell are ya?" Jimmy greeted him with surprise in his voice and a gratified look on his face. He reached over a stove that lay on its side next to the foundation wall and shook Jack's hand. "A couple of things before I get started here, guys. I checked into local snipers from the Vietnam era and came up with zero guys from Rhode Island. There were two guys in the New England area, but they came from the mountains up in God's country. I had to pull some big strings to get these guys' files. Luckily, someone owed me a big favor down at the armory, and he told me I'll have them on my desk by the end of the day."

"I guess that means I owe you a big favor now, right?" I said, smiling.

"I'm a cheap date, Elliot, and easy. A meal up on the Hill would be perfect."

"Whatever you want, James."

"Oh, one more thing, guys. The blood sample we grabbed on the stairs the other day is in, and there are no matches in the system." He looked around the scene. "Well, I guess I should get back to my job and stop bullshitting. Jack, great to see ya." Jimmy jumped back into the pile of junk like a kid in a sandbox.

The three of us walked around the neighboring area looking for anything out of the ordinary, but unfortunately we pulled up a net with no fish. We decided to take off and leave the excavating to Jimmy, his crew, and the fire department.

I had to get Jack back home, but before I did, I wanted to drop in and pay a visit to our East Coast real estate moguls and see what their game was.

"Hey, Sean," I said. "Do you remember the name of the company that owns the properties we're looking into?"

"Sure, VBG Properties. They have an office over on South Main Street, not too far from your house." Sean started the ignition and put his car into gear.

"I'm gonna see what they're all about, and then I'll see you later to go over the files and brush up on some paperwork."

Jack and I hopped in my car and followed Sean out of the rats' nest on the street.

"I'll tell ya, Jimmy will never change," Jack said. "He's nuts."

I chuckled. "Yeah, he's crazy. Smart bastard, though."

"God, yeah. ADD on every count, except paperwork."

We pulled up to the front door of VBG Properties, laughing about Jimmy Taylor's secretarial skills, and looked up, admiring the decadent entrance of the immaculate vintage building.

Jack came in with me to see what this company was all about. We walked in through the fancy entrance of the beautiful old brick building. The front doors, made of solid mahogany and etched glass, must have weighed 300 pounds apiece. The mammoth doors swung shut, and we stood in an empty lobby that was dressed and manicured like an actress at the Oscars.

A door opened at the top of a deluxe staircase that was more like a piece of elaborate furniture.

"Hello, gentleman. How can I help you?" A woman dressed to the nines in a business suit and stiletto heels stopped at the top step and then seductively slithered down the staircase. Jack grabbed his chest and stood there in awe, like a kid at the penny candy counter.

"We would like to speak to the person in charge." I respectfully unbuttoned my suit jacket and pulled it aside at my beltline, exposing my credentials.

"That would be Ms. Whitmore," she kindly responded. "Follow me, Detectives."

She brought Jack and me down a hallway that abutted the elaborate stairway's hand-carved spindles and garnished skirtboards. We followed her into an office that was nicer than my home.

She strolled behind the desk and sat down, and looked at us with a playful grin. "Sit down, Detectives," she invitingly suggested with her hands out and palms up.

Jack and I both thanked her with a nod and some small lip movements as we parked our seats in chairs I could have fallen into and slept in for a week.

She sat across from us, a stunning beauty with long blond hair, perfect teeth, and little rectangular glasses encased in a two-tone frame. "I'm Grace Whitmore," she said with an alluring smirk that I knew would get Jack's engine revved up and ready to race.

"Ms. Whitmore, we would like—"

She politely interrupted me. "Please, Detective. You can call me Grace."

"Okay, Grace. We're not here for any reason other than to inquire about some of your properties."

"Oh?" She turned her head, looking utterly fascinated, and then checked on her French manicure.

"What's the story with 26 Dean Street, next to the police station?"

"Would you like to purchase the property, um . . . I'm sorry, you never told me your name." Grace spoke with a spice that I knew was going to burn.

I responded politely, not wanting to push her buttons. "I'm sorry, Grace. I'm Elliot, and this is Jack."

"Would you like to purchase the property, Elliot?"

I played her game, knowing full well that she knew we weren't interested in buying the house. "No. I just want to know if you have any knowledge of anyone breaking into some of your abandoned buildings, or maybe living in them."

"Of course, Detectives. Most of the buildings we own are in much better neighborhoods, but some of these buildings get picked up in tax sales or foreclosures through our legal associates. Not my first choice, you see, but needless to say, money is money."

"I understand. I just want you to be aware that we've seen some action around these properties, and want to make sure they're secure." I repeated myself because she had totally avoided what I'd asked, knowing her money, power, and beauty would crush anything that I brought to the table.

"We've beefed up on our locks and security in the past year, especially because of the insurance companies, and for legal reasons. It has cost the company tens of thousands of dollars just here in Rhode Island, but there are always the exceptions who will chew through steel just to violate what isn't theirs. My brother and I are investing a lot of money in Providence, along with ten other major cities that span as far south as Florida." She flipped through a black leather planner and took out a business card.

"We just figured we'd stop by and get acquainted with VBG, seeing that we've been watching over some of your properties." I kept it simple for now, not wanting to enter onto her radar just yet.

"I'll be sure to bring my maintenance crew up to speed." She handed me her card, very unconcerned, and looked at her watch. "Oh, look at the time. Detectives, I apologize, but I have a three thirty I cannot be late for. I have a flight to catch tonight." She stood up, basically telling us to fuck off.

I stood up and shook her hand. "Thank you for your time." I turned around to walk out of her office and spotted a framed photograph of an army platoon hanging on the wall. "Wow, that's a cool picture."

"It belongs to my brother, Blake," she said in a melancholy tone as she swept us clean out of her office and toward the front door. "He was in Vietnam."

"I appreciate his service. Jack and I both served."

"That's nice. I'll be sure to tell my brother. I'm sure he'll appreciate the gesture."

Jack shook her hand and thanked Grace for her time, and their eyes hooked up for a second. Then we showed ourselves out. Back into reality, outside the offices of VBG, we got into the car and banged a steep right up John Street.

Jack filled me in with some history about the mesmerizing woman we had just left. "Grace's parents and sister were murdered at their home on Blackstone Boulevard in the summer of '75. She was just a young lady at the time, maybe early to mid-twenties, and absolutely stunning."

"Did they ever find the people who killed them?"

"Not that I know of, but I have to tell you something. You bringing up all this sniper talk and fresh evidence has been dredging up old memories, and makes me wonder if our perp went from a blade to a gun. Shortly after the Whitmores were murdered, a couple of guys got whacked with a big-caliber round. A couple of our older guys said they thought the shot had come from on top of a building, and that it was possibly a sniper. There was no evidence, nor did anyone bother to look past their noses, but the thought of revenge didn't cross anyone's mind, including mine, until now.

"The two schmucks who got snuffed had pocketsful of money on them and were figured for just fucking over the wrong somebody. We figured that someone might have been Pasquale 'Big Fingers' Nardo. The hit was a big deal for a day or two, but other cases came through the door and got dropped at our feet, and with no one crying over these two punks, it made it easy to turn the page on them. I think if you look at that particular case, it was written up as a Mob hit."

"So our boy might have slid right under the radar because he changed tactics . . . Did anyone question Blake at the time?"

"Grace and her brother were informed by officials in Florida at the family's home that very day of their death. I remember it like it was yesterday."

"They could've hired someone to do the job." The initial thoughts that had popped into my head fired out of my mouth. It was just pure instinct to ask questions that I was sure had been asked many, many times before.

"Yeah, they could have. But we'll never find that out." Jack pulled on the door handle as we rolled up to his house, and got out of the car. Some clouds drifted over us, hiding the sun, and he threw me a relaxed salute. "See ya, Elliot."

Chapter 10

I headed back to the station to hopefully pluck some of the keys off the keychain we'd collected while building this case. I pulled up to the station and looked at the sky. It was a dark charcoal, and looked evil and destructive. The sky lit up from above the parking garage, followed by a crash and a rumble that shook the ground. I got out just as oversized pellets of rain started slamming the car and the pavement below my feet. The distinct smell of cold, damp earth came through the air from the east as the rain fell in a heavier, tighter pattern and grew increasingly volatile. The parking lot turned white and greasy, shedding a knee-high steam that billowed around the consumed lot.

I bolted toward the building, getting soaked. Brian Verdi, one of our bicycle cops, held open the door, letting me make a smooth, quick entrance.

"Thank you!" I yelled out, almost hopping the entire curb before putting on the brakes.

"That seemed to come out of nowhere," Brian said.

"Yeah, no shit. I was wearing my sunglasses ten minutes ago. Thanks, Brian."

"No problem."

I walked to the locker room, soaked to the bone. I always kept a spare suit at the station, just in case. After changing and grabbing a hot cup of coffee from the machine, I headed to find Sean and Jimmy. I found them together in Jimmy's office, working on the new leads.

Sean turned around and sized me up. "What'd you do, change your suit?"

"Yeah, I just got caught in that downpour." I set my coffee down on a corner of the table they'd been working at. "So, what do we have so far?"

"We've got everything that's happened in the past couple of days," Sean said. "But we really have to organize it."

The three of us decided it was a perfect day to stay indoors and put some time in on the details of what we'd collected. When you're after a perp with a level of complexity that outlines the outlines, everything becomes about the details. Only your animal instinct can hold on to and track the scent of such a paramount figure's footsteps.

"We just need one small slipup to bring us within striking distance," Sean declared.

I scooped up numerous piles from the table, where they'd laid everything out, and flipped through them. "I'll start clipping everything up on the board."

"If you need pushpins, they're in the bottom drawer." Jimmy pointed to his desk, which was being used as an open filing cabinet.

Sean and I got everything organized and posted up onto one of the walls. We mapped everything out, and included files on all VBG Properties locations around the city.

"I'm gonna go check to see if anything's arrived on that veteran from up north," Sean said.

I grabbed my phone and looked at the time. "I'm gonna check up on Meg. See how she's doing." I took a walk down the hall and called my future sister-in-law. "Hey, Denise. How is she?"

"There's really no change, Elliot. Everything is pretty much the same."

"I'll be in as soon as I get a break. Just tell her I love her, okay?"

"I will. I don't want you to feel bad. There's really not much you can do here at this point."

"I know, but you know how it is."

Denise sighed. "I know. That's why I'm telling you to just do what you need to do."

"Okay, thanks. I'll talk to you later."

"Okay. 'Bye, Elliot."

I walked back to Jimmy's office and realized he had also left. I sighed deeply, taking in the rare quiet moment alone, and tried to shake off my thoughts of Megan.

Sean came in soon after, carrying a big manila envelope. "How is she? Any change?"

"Her vitals are stable, but she's still the same."

Sean tapped my shoulder. "She's going to pull through, man. Everything's gonna work out."

"Thanks, bud." I pointed to the envelope Sean was holding. "Is that his file?" Although I was caught up in my overcast feelings, I couldn't wait to see what the file had to say.

"Yup." Sean slid the paperwork across the table. "Let's check it out and see if anything slaps us in the face."

I shook the file out in front of us. Sean and I split the file, reading the small chunk of information on a Mr. Steve Krasson's military time. This particular soldier had been born in Providence, but at the age of eight, he lost both his parents and moved to Vermont to live with his uncle. His service time was extremely impressive—a Silver Star, two Bronze Stars for valor, and what looked like the Congressional Medal of Honor, but it had been blacked out along with two-thirds of his records. It looked as if he'd been involved in a lot of hush-hush missions, since they were all stamped CLASSIFIED and blacked out.

"This guy Krasson is a war hero." Sean put down the paperwork he had on our one lead for a possible suspect. "He stayed in Vietnam for almost four years."

I lifted my head up from the piece I'd been staring at and scanning over and over. "What year did his last tour end?"

"Uh, let's see." Sean scanned down the page. "It says here he enlisted in 1965 and came home in 1969."

"In '69, huh? Is there anything on his marital status?"

"No, but listen to this. He joined when he was only eighteen years old. And on his birthday, of all days." Sean and I looked at each other, a bit confused.

"His birthday? Christ, did he sleep in his clothes that night waiting for the bus to drive him straight into war? Hey, whatever, I guess he just wanted out of Vermont." I stared at the file, wondering what kind of sadness this guy Steve Krasson had been through, losing both of his parents at such a young age.

"It also says he was picked for sniper training right out of boot camp," Sean said. "There's a letter attached to his certificate of graduation. *Paris Island, South Carolina, Platoon 284.* The letter states, *The United States Marine Corps will have a brief holding of Steve Krasson, Private, E-1, for deployment to Vietnam, to undergo sniper training due to his extraordinary shooting and combat skills*, recommend by a Gunnery Sergeant Alan."

I was a bit dazzled with Mr. Krasson's file. "Because so much of his file is painted black and stamped confidential, it leads me to believe he was working for the CIA."

"Okay, why don't we see if he's in the system? This guy could be dead, for all we know."

"Hey, it's worth a shot. If he's not going to leave us with any forensic trail, maybe he has a paper one."

While Sean profiled Steve Krasson, I sat there looking at the piles, pictures, and nailed-up facts on the board, trying to group together the mess that lay everywhere.

Jimmy darted into the room. "Elliot, you're never going to believe it."

"Surprise me, Jimmy."

"I just figured you'd want to know that the stiffs from the meth explosion were executed in the ear socket, just like the others."

"You gotta be shitting me." I almost fell over from the slider that Jimmy had delivered up my ass.

"What about the explosion?" Sean asked.

"The fire department thinks the kitchen stove ignited high levels of acetone that had filled the house up like a fog."

"So, wait a minute, Jimmy," I said. "Let me get this right. What you're telling me is that our perp put down the three meth cookers with his signature move, and then, on his way out, he fired on the gas stove, using it like a big cigarette lighter, and blew the place to shit, making it look like a meth accident."

"Yep. That sounds about right." Jimmy laughed at the crazy and ingenious plot our perp, whoever he was, had leveled off right in front of our eyes. "Oh, and one more thing. The two maggots who hit Megan's bank did the inside job alone. The surveillance recordings show only the two deceased punks inside the bank."

"So again, the driver got close enough to earn their trust," I said, shaking my head. "He befriended them, like all his victims. He's a fucking full-blown vigilante! You were right."

Sean looked at me as Steve Krasson's records popped up on the screen. We all gazed at the computer, trying to focus on the only suspect we had.

"Well, unless he's a ghost, it's not Krasson," Sean said. "Looks like he passed away in 1975. He received a full military funeral at Arlington Cemetery."

"Does it say how or where he died?" I asked.

Jimmy squinted at the antiquated screen, trying to get around the glare of the fluorescents. "It says here that he drowned after he lost control of his vehicle and ended up in the drink down in Walton County."

My brow furrowed. "Where the hell is Walton County?"

"It's down in the panhandle, close to Panama City, Florida," Jimmy stated matter-of-factly.

"Leave it to you to know that, Taylor," Sean replied.

"My parents have a place on the beach south of there. I've actually driven through Walton County before. When you get inland, it's very quiet. I'm sure back in the late '70s, it must've been desolate."

"Or maybe a great place to hide," I said.

"So I guess we have to assume this guy Krasson isn't our guy, if he's six feet deep in Arlington cemetery," Sean said.

"The key word, there, is 'assume,'" Jimmy said. "I don't want any of us to end up with egg on our face or get jammed up. Shit with veterans can get a little touchy."

"Do me a favor," I said to Sean. "Look into a Grace Whitmore, and see what you can find out—married, single, widowed, all her siblings. Also, find out about her brother. When you get the whole scoop on her, call me."

"Guys, I gotta go take a dump, and then I'm gonna hit my hiding spot for some leftover Chinese." Jimmy disappeared from his office and headed down the quiet hallway.

Sean jumped right in on Grace and worked his finger magic on the keyboard.

I tapped the side of the monitor on the way out the door. "See ya, bud."

"Take care," Sean said. "I'll talk to you shortly."

Chapter 11

On my drive to T. F. Green Airport, I dropped a line to a high school pal, Ken Sast, who worked for the airport police. I asked him to check to see if there was a bird scheduled to fly out with my new friend, Grace Whitmore, on board, and if so, where she was flying to and whether any guests would be joining her.

I was less than ten minutes from the airport, waiting on hold for Ken's report, when Sean beeped in. My mind started racing, wondering what his phone call might entail. I had to answer. I clicked over, ending my one-person conversation for the moment.

I answered the call on the edge of my seat. "Did you find something?"

"Well, I found Grace, along with her family tree, but they're all deceased except her brother, Blake."

"Ever married? Kids?"

"Not that I can see." He talked as he skimmed through the information on his screen. "Born 1954, Providence, Rhode Island. Parents, Ronald and Julia Whitmore, along with younger sister, Victoria Whitmore, deceased, 1975. Brother, Blake Whitmore, alive and well."

"Does she have any other living family?"

"Negative."

"Hold on, Sean. I have to take this call. Just gimme one minute." I clicked over to answer Ken's delayed call.

"Hey, Ken. I'm sorry. I had to take another call. What did you find out?" I asked hurriedly, as I was getting closer to the airport every second.

"Grace is boarding a Cessna in roughly thirty minutes, with a Blake Whitmore."

"I'll be there in ten minutes." I looked at the green time display on the radio, then smashed the gas pedal and dropped down a gear.

"Listen, Elliot, park up front where the passenger vans park. I'll meet you at the main entrance."

"I'll see you there, Ken." I clicked back and returned my attention to Sean. "I'm sorry, man. Continue."

"The funny thing is, the intermission gave me some more time to study the Whitmore clan."

"What else did you find out?"

"Her brother, Blake, is a Vietnam vet. He was honorably discharged with a Purple Heart in '69."

"Well, that's interesting. Does it say why he was discharged? Does it say if he was a sniper?"

"No. I'm actually grabbing this info from a *Providence Journal* article that was done on VBG about fifteen years back. I'm sure we can do a little digging on Blake and pull up some history that's been buried away." Sean crunched on a chip or a cracker in my ear.

"Keep digging, Sean. I'll call you back later." I ended the call, seeing Ken waiting at the front entrance. *How could a woman that beautiful be single?* I asked myself while getting out of the car.

I walked over with my hand out. Ken reciprocated and greeted me with a handshake and half a hug.

"Follow me." Ken held the door open for me and started walking through the busy terminal. He picked up the pace and hooked us up with a shortcut so we wouldn't have to deal with the carousel and baggage claim bullshit.

"Where's this flight headed?" I inquired as I jumped up the stairs to the control tower, trying to keep up.

"Carson County Airport," he replied, grabbing some papers off a desk in the control tower. "C'mon. This way."

We walked to the glass overlooking the airstrips, and I flipped through the manifest Ken had given to me.

"As you can see," Ken said, "Blake and Grace fly up and down the East Coast nonstop."

I asked Ken if he could give me a heads-up when they were in the air back to Rhode Island. I looked out across the strip at all the busy hustle and bustle while Ken talked with his buddy in air traffic. He gave me the thumbs-up for the Whitmores' arrival back into the Ocean State.

"Thanks, Ken. I really appreciate you doing this for me."

Ken nodded. "There's the Cessna," he said, pointing straight ahead at the small blue-and-white luxury jet that was ready and waiting for takeoff. He grabbed some binoculars off the giant sill and handed them to me.

I wasted no time holding them up to my eyes. I pointed the yard goggles in the direction of the plane and focused them on the stairs that led into the jet. I looked at my watch and asked Ken when they would board.

He looked at his watch. "They're due to take off in ten minutes."

I didn't want to start reminiscing with Ken and end up burning the eggs, so I watched my objective closely and kept my mouth shut.

Ken was checking with one of his guys on the radio about covering for another officer who had called in sick, when I finally saw them glide onto the tarmac. I raised the field glasses back to my eyes and followed them to the bird. They were traveling light, with only one carry-on apiece strapped over their shoulders.

Grace was as polished as a vintage Ferrari, and looked even more beautiful than when we had met. Blake wore pitch-black sunglasses and was dressed casually, with his hair greased back and a heavy scruff on his face that made him look a little out of place when he stood near Grace.

As they got to the airstairs, Blake moved aside and allowed Grace to board the jet first. She acknowledged him with a smile and a pat on the cheek as she passed by and made her way aboard the vessel. He followed her up the bridge and into the aircraft, and the door shut behind them.

Before I could make sense of all the thoughts in my head about these two, the aircraft blew down the runway and lifted off the ground, and flew away into the dusk. They disappeared into the early evening sky, leaving me with a headful of scenarios that I thought Ken would surely be able to see leaking out of my ears.

I lowered the glasses and handed them back to Ken while I thanked him for all his help. Then I navigated my way back to the fire lane where I had left my seat and four wheels.

I hopped into my ride and headed back toward the station, hoping that Sean and Jimmy had dug a trench from here to Walton County.

~~~

I rolled back into the city and was approaching the off-ramp when a house break and possible domestic abuse call came across the radio. I was just a couple of minutes away from the call, so I decided to lend a hand. I hit the lights, took the exit, and punched it up the incline.

I made it to the scene in less than two minutes and found a patrol car already there. I pulled up in front of the address, parallel to the curb. Charlie Lee, a senior patrolman I knew very well, was across the street, looking up into the top apartment. I hopped out and sprinted across the street to see what Charlie knew about the call.

He gave me the skinny on the situation immediately. "Apparently, the asshole upstairs just got out of prison yesterday and is holding his ex-girlfriend at knifepoint. He says he's going to kill her and her baby." Charlie pointed up at the third floor window, where you could hear a loud argument and some crying.

"That's right, motherfuckers," the ex-boyfriend yelled out the window, waving a large kitchen knife. "I'm gonna stick her and the little brat. The bitch couldn't wait just two years for me. She had to go out and start a family without me, and now I'm gonna end that." He growled with rage and violence like a rabid animal, screamed into the early evening air, and then turned back into the apartment.

I could hear him slapping the shit out of the woman. I looked around at the surrounding houses. They were quiet, out of the madness for the moment.

"Come on, man," Charlie hollered back up to him. "You don't want to do that. Let them go, and let us help you out of this." He tried being diplomatic. He didn't want to piss the guy off.

With no warning, the window the ex-con had been yelling out of blew into the air with utter destruction and smashed all over the police cars on the street below.

"This guy's gonna kill 'em!" Charlie exclaimed.

I looked back up at the window, and a box came flying out, perfectly level, as if it had been fired from a slingshot, and sailed through the heavy night air. "Look out, Charlie!"

Charlie covered his head.

Smash!

An old-school wood-grain microwave oven landed on Charlie's patrol car, caving in the entire hood.

"What the fuck!" Charlie screamed. "This car's brand-new!"

The maniac howled out the window. "The little brat's next! Little bitch is gonna learn how to fly."

The woman's screams and her helpless baby's wails from inside the apartment filled up the neighborhood with terror.

"Fuck it, we have no time!" I shouted. I walked to the rear of my unmarked and grabbed the long gun that I still had sequestered in the trunk.

I looked around, trying to be as inconspicuous as possible, ran across the street, and vanished down a dark alley as two more cruisers pulled up. I scampered around in the gloom, navigating around garbage cans. I cut through the thick, clammy night air like a knife and had to wipe the sweat off my face with my sleeve more than once. The beads of sweat on my forehead got bigger and heavier, running into my eyes and making it more difficult to see than it already was.

I came across a fire escape attached to the side of a brick building. I looked back to where I had come from, trying to assess my chances of a clear poke from twenty-five feet above where I stood. I could still hear the maniac's threats. With no time left, I made my decision to climb up and see if I'd have an attainable shot. I threw the rod over my shoulder, jumped up, and pulled down the ladder that I'd have to scale to get to my roost.

I climbed up that rickety piece of shit, stopped at the third and last floor, and swung the gun off my shoulder. I estimated my distance at roughly seventy-five yards and crouched down, resting my hand on a metal rail that was covered in bird shit. I targeted the house where the man was still screaming and pulled focus on the reprobate in my lens.

The newly freed inmate was holding on to the infant's shirt as she hung in midair, swinging around like a net full of oranges, while he waved a kitchen knife in his other hand. He screamed and pointed his blade at the mother, who was crying her eyes out and begging him to stop.

I adjusted the scope to pull off this short poke. Before I could take a shot, the unhinged parolee decided he was done talking and gave his ex a front ball kick, sending her flying through the air away from the window and out of my sight. The madman turned around, approached the broken casement, and cocked his arm back softball style, ready to lob the little baby girl out of the window and into the arms of the Grim Reaper. In a flash, I perceived his intentions, which he narrated to me through the violence in his eyes.

I exhaled through my nose with intent, plucked back the hair trigger, and picked him off. Completely unaware of the clean, painless headshot made by the NATO round, the inmate simply collapsed to his knees and fell backward. I saw the boys come blasting in and flood the tiny apartment like a tsunami within seconds. I watched them through the high-powered scope as they stood inspecting the abstract piece painted on the wall by the contents of the convict's head.

Charlie bent down, grabbed the baby girl, and walked to the window. He looked out from the horror show into the night, and sighed with relief that she and her mother were alive.

I climbed down the fire escape and got my feet on the ground. I headed back, hoping I wouldn't arrive on the red carpet. When I got back to the street, lit up from one end to the other with oscillating red and blue lights, I looked down at my suit. It was trashed and completely soaked from my little excursion. I stayed tight to any fixed structure I could find and glided to my car, trying to remain invisible.

I hid away my tool of destruction, closed the trunk, and looked around to see if anyone across the street from the crime scene could have witnessed what had really happened. Charlie walked out the front door of the building, guiding the mother. She was all smashed up and could barely walk. He brought her to the ambulance that had just arrived. The paramedics leaped out, spooled up with adrenaline, and helped Charlie get the mother and daughter aboard the hospital wagon.

I climbed the stairs to the apartment and walked in to have a peek. The ghetto penthouse was trashed, flipped upside down, and held my targeted kill within the four pastel peach-colored walls of its parlor. He bled out on the oak floor as he lay there with his eyes wide open.

I looked up at the light show that consumed my immediate focus and trained my vision past it all, into the field of darkness where I had been lurking. As sick as it was, I understood that my vigilante perp was trying to wipe out the disease from the snot-filled streets of this city.

I left the apartment and bumped into Charlie on my way out the door at the bottom of the stairs.

Charlie put his hand on my shoulder. "That little girl would be dead if you hadn't taken the measures you did, Elliot, and that's what I'm putting in my report, along with everyone else here," he said, trying to validate my murdering the asshole upstairs, who would require a closed-casket funeral thanks to me, and reassure me of my innocence.

"Thanks, man, I appreciate it. I'm sure I'm gonna need as many people backing me as possible." I looked out the door to the growing number of spectators quickly filling up the area. "I'd better go, Charlie. I'll talk with you later on."

I headed out and got into my car. I was about to pull the door shut when I heard my name.

"Hey, Elliot!"

I turned back to the house and saw Charlie still standing in the front door.

"Hey, I'm really glad you were two minutes down the road," he said and smiled.

I threw him two fingers off my forehead in salute. Then I backed up and drove away.

~~~

I got back to the station and scooped off the passenger's seat the dozen wieners and coffee milks I'd grabbed at New York System along the way. I walked into the station, which was unusually quiet, down the empty hall, and into Jimmy's office. I threw the bag of dogs on the table and sat down, my head spinning with uncertainty over my recent vigilante act.

It looked as if the guys had done some serious excavating on the

Whitmore bloodline while I'd been gone. There was a lot of new info posted up on the case board, and fresh printouts were scattered around the table in organized piles, along with some new and old clutter.

"You read my mind," Jimmy said.

The boys wasted no time unwinding the greasy white paper that wrapped up the dogs in threes and dug in, dropping meat sauce and onions onto the table, various parts of their clothing, and the floor. Working with the right guys was always key, and made the time pass with certain pleasures. In the past, I'd been stuck with some real nitwits. Some of those guys couldn't detect a fart in a phone booth.

I explained my airport visit, and also what had happened on my ride back to the boys.

Sean shook his head. "Hey, what were you supposed to do?"

"Exactly," Jimmy said. "Sounds to me like all three of them would be dead if you hadn't stepped in."

"Maybe . . . ," I said, still unsure of myself. "But enough of that. It looks like you guys hit it hard while I was gone."

"I've traced the Whitmore name back to the Industrial Revolution." Sean crinkled up his wrapper full of onions and hit the trash for three points. "We're talking about old money, my friend."

"That doesn't surprise me in the least. Wealth and attitude radiate off this woman like a fine vintage wine. But I gotta tell ya, her brother doesn't carry around the same feeling of affluence. He looks like a rough and tough bastard, a different breed."

"Speaking of Blake, I called in another favor and found out about his discharge." Jimmy told me the news as he finished his three-pack, plus one of mine. "In '69, his platoon got ambushed. Everyone got wiped out except him and three others. The North Vietnamese Army took the four of them as prisoners for thirteen weeks. They were all severely tortured, but miraculously were saved. All of them were honorably discharged because of the conditions they had undergone. So Blake not only had his family ripped away, but he also suffers with the terror of the war and the POW camp sticking in his side."

Before I could get a word in, Sean hit me with another shot, this time a left hook. "And there's one more thing, Elliot. Do you remember our friend Mr. Krasson? The sniper who's buried in Arlington?"

"Of course. What did you find out?"

"I got in touch with the Walton County Sheriff's Department, and they looked up his accident. They told me the report said that his body was never found, but that his car went off the road into alligator-infested waters. They retrieved his wallet and some clothing that they pulled away from the gators."

"Holy shit. Fuckin' guy does close to four tours in 'Nam, and gets taken down by some gators."

"Elliot, can I talk to you for a minute?" Major Sullivan interjected, drifting into our crime lab on a breeze.

"Sure, Major." I looked to the boys and then stepped out into the hallway, certain that Sullivan's visit was to take me out of the game. "Are you here to suspend me?"

"No, not yet. I'm actually just giving you a heads-up that Internal Affairs will need your statement and full report to correspond with the other information they've already gathered on this incident. In my opinion, I'd say you're in the clear. There are too many witnesses, including all our guys' statements, saying the two victims would be dead if you hadn't acted on impulse. But you know how it works. These guys have a hard-on for you right now. Worst-case scenario, maybe a small suspension with pay." He shrugged his shoulders.

"No problem, Major. I'll have it done by tomorrow." I walked back into the room as Sullivan took off for the night. "Well, that's a big load off my brain."

The boys congratulated me on the good news, happy to see that the suits wouldn't be stoning me in the courtyard just yet. We continued with our research, speculations, and assumptions, putting our experience and some long hours into the case that we thought might just go down in history.

Chapter 12

Grace Whitmore opened the door to their beautiful Dutch Colonial. It had no ocean views, but was located just twenty minutes from Santa Rosa Beach. The family home, which Grace had spent a lot of time in as a young girl, was surrounded by perennial gardens and hardscapes that belonged in a Martha Stewart photo shoot. The traditional stonework and unique design of the house had that delicate but old-world touch that wowed most people who saw it for the first time. The estate had been in the Whitmore name since the early nineteenth century, and had become a sort of getaway, or even a home base, for the members of the family who used it.

Blake took their bags and put them away down the bedroom corridor, while Grace grabbed two martini glasses out of the antique cherry liquor cupboard along with an unopened bottle of vodka. She watched Blake as he strolled back and sat down in the sunroom, getting comfortable. He stared back at her through his jet black wraparound Harry Callahan shades.

Grace poured the vodka from a jigger onto the Spanish olives waiting to be drenched with alcohol. "Beautiful olives," she said absently, gazing past the drinks on the enormous marble countertop to Blake, who stared out the glass room overlooking the historic property.

Grace walked across the open kitchen and stepped down into the sunken sunroom, joining Blake, and handed over the perfectly made dirty martini. She looked over the same grounds, with reflections of her childhood cascading before her eyes—summers, Christmas vacations, her grandparents telling stories to the family, neighborhood friends, cookouts, big white tents full of guests, ghost stories, sleepovers, campfires.

Grace's smile didn't last long, as happy memories turned to thoughts of melancholy and pain. "They were all taken too young, especially Victoria."

Blake sat and stared out the same window, like a chamberstick with no candle. "I know."

An uneasy feeling came over her, an obvious sadness tied to separation, certain dates, and meaningful history. She tipped back the glass and took in a bigger mouthful, and watched her drinking buddy, who was haunted by his own memories.

Over the course of an hour, more than half the bottle had been poured. The hundred-proof cocktails became smoother, and the subject of why they were getting cocked became clearer.

The bottle fell toward empty as Grace read through the mental list of her loved ones who were gone and who visited her like ghosts in the night. The flooding alcohol warmed her wounds and encouraged her to change channels. She stood up and had to catch herself from falling off-kilter. Her booze intake had been accompanied by only an English muffin and some dark-roast coffee that she'd had at breakfast almost five hours before.

She was feeling loose, so she unbuttoned her suit jacket, shed it off onto the chair where she sat, and let her hair down. She seductively flipped open the buttons on her white fitted blouse, but left it on, with her pastel pink bra and firm abdomen exposed. She stepped in front of him and took off his dark shades, revealing eyes full of obsession, hypnotized by her sexual spell. She put on the tinted lenses, flipped her blond hair back, and climbed onto his lap. Her skirt rode up her legs and hugged tight to the tops of her thighs. She ran her fingers through his thick, slicked-back salt-and-pepper hair as he clenched one mitt tightly on to her panty line and grabbed the upper lace of her nude thigh-highs with the other hand.

"Make love to me, Blake," Grace said with a playful laugh that was embellished by the alcohol. She felt her juices let go as she buried her head into his and smelled the scruff of his neck and his hair.

"What did I tell you about calling me that when we make love?" Steve Krasson shouted as he pulled away and looked straight into her eyes.

"I'm sorry," Grace replied without hesitation or defense, understanding that her joke had not been funny. She ran her fingers behind his ear while tilting her head like a cute puppy dog that had been scolded.

He stared at her as if it was the first time their eyes had met, totally understanding one another's pain. "Call me by my real name," Steve said with a soft but stern tone in his voice. He handled the situation perfectly, without disturbing the natural moment between the two lovers.

She hopped on his notion, getting more and more excited because of their hidden secret. "Please, Mr. Krasson, make love to me," Grace pleaded, grabbing his button-down polo and tugging on it as if she was starting an engine.

"That's more like it." Steve grabbed her waist tightly with a rough right grip and a ball of her hair with his left. He squeezed her passionately in his powerful hands and drew her into him. His power and aggression opened her up. He kissed her and dragged his lips all over her neck and down the middle of her chest. He removed her blouse, letting it fall to the floor, and unclipped her bra. He buried his head between her breasts, and she grabbed the back of his head and held him close.

Grace arched her back and tilted her head, looking at the ceiling in utter bliss as Providence's most wanted man, Steve Krasson, went to work on his lover of almost forty years. They both knew that their little secret dragged the sexual intensity of their relationship to a different altitude. Their terrain was much different from the working nine-to-five, picking up the rug rats, fanning through the same bills again and again, eating meatloaf, matching La-Z-Boy recliners, pajama pants, litter box stink, "Mom, the goldfish is in the toilet," "Make sure you brush your teeth," and "Shh, be quiet, the kids will hear!" kind of life.

Grace screamed out with pleasure and rattled the jalousie windows. Steve's entire body tensed up with the self-satisfaction that he was her superman, her one and only, and she was his reason for not diving off the tightwire he walked every day.

Chapter 13

Jack and I had just finished Sunday breakfast and sat sipping our tallboy Bloody Marys on his porch and talking.

I looked to him for some advice on how to make it to twenty years on the job. "How did you stay on the force for forty years?"

"I don't know, to be honest with you, kid. I guess it just made me feel alive." Jack seemed pensive as he looked up at the mahogany beadboard ceiling. "I can't believe I'm retired and looking at seventy in a few years."

"I know. Time really does fly, doesn't it?"

"It only gets faster the older you get, believe me."

I pushed my empty plate toward the center of the table and placed my drink in front of me. "IID is gonna chew my ass off for shooting that jerk."

Jack tipped back his glass and finished up his second drink. "Oh, fuck them. There's only one true way to get scum off the street. I guess I probably wouldn't last twenty hours if I had to do it all over again." Jack started to laugh with a gleam of craziness in his eyes.

"Sometimes I think I'd rather work with our perp than some of these robots over at the station, you know?"

"Yeah, I know what you're talking about, kid. The bureaucratic bullshit ruins, but also runs, most of the job these days. No one can just use common sense anymore to make a decision. They all sprint to the extreme cases with their noses buried in the pages of the law, until they eventually fuck the good guy and blow the bad guy."

"The attorney general's office and state police are looking into my case, but Major Sullivan feels I'll be cleared with all the witnesses, and of course because of the nature of the situation with that dirtbag."

"Fuck that guy. He's out of jail for a day and chooses to take out a baby. What were you suppose to do, let him kill two innocent people?"

"Sometimes you might be better off. Now I'm knee-deep in shit."

"Come on, you know you wouldn't change a thing. We're in the business of protecting people from scum like that."

"No, you're right. I wouldn't."

"Listen, I've been in your shoes. That convict prick got what he deserved." Jack pushed back his chair and got up to make another batch of the drinks that were making me want to stay on his front porch all day.

I chopped at the ice in my glass with a celery stick, thinking about Blake and Grace and what they were doing right then. Were they responsible for the murders that I was currently investigating? Or did I have the hounds barking up the wrong tree?

The screen door swung open, and out came Jack with a pitcher full of the spicy red elixir that was helping to ease the current strain on my broad shoulders.

I looked up at him as he refilled our glasses. "Jack, I have nine dead people and a pocketful of speculation on this killer. Maybe some of my suspicions are just . . . nothing."

"Listen, if I've told you once, I've told you a thousand times—a good amount of police work is speculation and acting on your gut feelings." Jack sat down and stirred his drink with a leafy celery shoot. "You may not have enough to point the finger just yet, but something inside of you knows there are certain things that just don't add up. I think you're on the right path. I can feel it, and I think you can, too. And I have a sneaking suspicion that whoever's running from you is sleeping with one eye open."

"I know what this guy has done is wrong, if we go by the book, but he served revenge for me by killing those two fuckheads involved with the bank job. So, really, what's the difference between him and us? If I caught them, I was going to kill them myself. I played it out in my mind when I was chasing after them."

"The badge you carry around is the only difference."

"Yeah, I know. Sometimes it feels like it's all bullshit."

"Listen, kid, I'm not going to sit here and preach to you about ethics, because I'm the last one who should teach that lesson. There are people who called me a vigilante and wanted to send me to Mars when I was on the job. In some ways, I was. But when your garbage can starts to smell, you take it out, and in a way, that's what this guy's doing. The problem is, the law doesn't allow that, and unfortunately, you're on the side that enforces those laws. So unless your perp is hiring and has a great medical plan, I'd say you don't have much choice but to stay with the department and put up with the bullshit."

Nearly two houses down and speaking in falsetto, we got our daily greeting. "Good morning!" Janice waved energetically as she moved up the road with an extra step in her morning power walk.

"Morning, Janice." I looked at the time on my watch, realizing I should go to the hospital before the whole day disappeared.

"Why don't you join us in a little relaxation?" Jack stood up and held his tall glass in an invitation that veered her off the straight line of curb and across to the front steps.

Janice held her hips, deciding between the invitation she'd been waiting for and the rest of her morning ritual. She smiled nervously. "Let me go home and change out of these sweaty clothes."

Jack waved his hand for her to join us. "Come on, what fun is that?"

"I don't know, Jack, my hair isn't done, and I'm not wearing any makeup."

"You don't need that stuff. Look at you, you're gorgeous. Now get up here, take a break, and have a drink with us."

Jack's smooth compliments made her giggle, and she blushed, turning a couple shades of red deeper than what her power walk had already brought out. She hesitated for a few seconds and then laughed, knowing she'd lost the battle. "Okay, Jack, you twisted my arm."

I stood up and downed what was left lingering in the ice at the bottom of my glass. "I gotta go, guys. I'm sorry, but I really need to check on Megan."

"Okay, Elliot. I'll see ya later." Jack didn't put up a fight for me to hang around. He shook my hand and turned his focus to the hot little number wearing skin-tight yoga pants and a matching, equally tight tank top.

Chapter 14

Steve walked back from Blake's grave, holding Grace's hand. They had buried him long ago at the south end of the parklike grounds and marked his grave with a chunk of granite that Steve had found in one of the antique stone walls that bordered the eighty acres. Steve had dug the hole and buried him under some of the oldest trees on the property. It was a cool and secluded area, and had also been Blake's favorite drinking spot.

Steve remembered how Grace and he had taken care of Blake right up until his death. The mental state the Vietnam War had left him with had done him in, and neither the booze nor Blake's one-hour sessions with his shrink, Dr. Sweet, nor Grace's love and compassion, nor Steve, his savior, could help draw that poison out of him. Blake had died in the fall of 1975 from alcohol poisoning, just months after his parents and baby sister were murdered.

On the walk back to the house, Steve watched as Grace picked some fresh grapefruit and oranges to go along with the eggs and grits she was going to cook for breakfast.

When they got back to the house, Steve sat outside on the patio, surrounded by the rich colors that illuminated a picture of beauty, an abstruse contrast of his world. He drifted off into his subconscious, thinking about Blake and how much he had suffered as a prisoner of the North Vietnamese in that camp just south of Cambodia.

Steve blamed himself for not finding the platoon sooner and thought maybe Blake wouldn't have been stripped down to the bone if he had found the camp maybe a week earlier. The day Steve had found them being tortured, the skies turned black and covered the concentration camp like a curtain of carnage and sheer destruction, wiping out the enemy clean from existence. The NVA soldiers all plummeted to murky depths, drowning in the bottomless inhumanity that they themselves had created.

When Steve rescued what was left of Blake and his men, he pulled them out of a hell that had held them within inches of crossing over to their mortality. Unfortunately, the infestation was too far gone, and these American soldiers, including Blake, were scarred with tattoos of Vietnam that eventually poisoned every last one of them.

Steve remembered Blake getting all liquored up under the trees where he now rested. He would share stories of murder and the torture that he and the other men who were captured had suffered, and no one recognized that pain better than Steve Krasson.

~~~

Grace watched Steve as he sat there encased in his world of broken souls lost to the Vietnam War and his varnished childhood that had been stripped of all its sheen and luster. She looked at him with love and compassion, understanding that the government, and people like her father, used Steve for his talents of dissolving people they didn't want around.

Steve needed the warmth and understanding that Grace gave to him, and taking care of him actually kept her in balance. He had placed her upon a pedestal a long time ago, a pedestal built from the sadness in both their lives that had made her the superwoman she was today.

Grace realized she probably would have been institutionalized from depression without Steve's mental atrophy to care for. She played back how she'd fallen in love with Steve and how much her brother had cared for him. There had been days when Blake would have complete meltdowns, and Steve was like the medicine that drew the venom out, giving Blake hope in his life.

When Blake had died unexpectedly, Grace constructed the plan of switching Blake's and Steve's identities to protect Steve from the law, keeping him close to the roots, well below the deadly blades. Grace knew it would take any heat that might possibly come Steve's way and send the searchers looking somewhere else. Grace couldn't bear the thought of losing her newfound love, especially from doing her father's dirty work.

She remembered wedging Steve's wallet with his credentials into the driver's seat, so the crash wouldn't break it free. Grace and Steve had sent the car with nobody in it down into the alligator-infested drinking hole with all the windows rolled down.

When the police had pulled up the car, but no driver, they noticed the alligators floating on the sidelines, surrounding some clothes that were wrapped up in the alligator weed. That in itself closed the case, breaking any red flags for foul play that were brought up by the local authorities.

Her plan had been flawless, but ever since Detective Frantallo had thrown the burner below them on simmer, their feet were starting to burn enough to change the viscosity of their daily flow.

Grace plated up breakfast with the proper garnishes and placement, making their meal look beautiful, like everything she touched. She turned on the television and put on the news, and called Steve over to sit with her and eat. Steve joined her and dug into a breakfast that could have been prepared by some fancy hotel on Martha's Vineyard.

Breaking news from Rhode Island took Steve off the food highway he was cruising down and brought his attention to the television.

"Oh, now what?" Grace said as she looked at the television and then at Steve.

"Last night, in Providence, an inmate who had been released from the Adult Correctional Institute just yesterday morning was shot and killed. We'll be back in a minute with the details." The news anchor handed the floor over to the weatherman, who gave a quick rundown of the seven-day forecast.

The news flash forced Grace to take a few mental steps back to recheck the view. She knew it had something to do with that detective. And she knew that detective might be a splinter that could cause a serious infection.

The news anchor came back, which pulled her focus back to the screen. "We're back. The breaking news story comes to us from Providence, Rhode Island. Last night, an inmate who was discharged early yesterday from the Adult Correctional Institute in Cranston was shot when he allegedly tried to throw a baby out of a third-floor apartment window.

"A Providence police detective who showed up on the scene, and whose name has not been released, shot the inmate, Luther Brice, age thirty-six, with a sniper rifle. Witnesses say if the young detective hadn't used these harsh and cowboy-like measures, the baby girl and her mother would both be dead.

"No charges are being brought on the detective at this time. We will hear from some witnesses who were there at the scene last night and who think the police detective is a true hero."

"He's a hero," a woman who lived across the street told a news reporter. She stood in her front door, wearing a head full of curlers and 1950s-style thick Coke-bottle glasses. "I saw the whole thing from my apartment."

"Frantallo might end up being a problem." Steve turned from the television, totally blocking out the broadcast. He chewed on his crispy piece of bacon and hopped back onto the highway that he had earlier taken a detour from.

Grace started to clean up their interrupted breakfast after shutting off the TV.

Steve bit the end off of his short, chunky maduro and lit it up. Thick smoke wafted into the air. "We're gonna have to start being very careful. This one has become too close to the whole situation because of those two assholes and what they did to his girl."

Grace thought about their return trip back to the Ocean State and what changes might have to be made to send Frantallo sniffing around someone else's shit pile. She got up with the loaded tray of dishes. "I'll pack up all of our stuff." She knew they had to cut their trip short and get back to the hot spot.

"Yeah, I think it's important to be in Providence right now." Steve got up and walked to the edge of the concrete patio. "We need to stay close to our new friend, Elliot Frantallo."

Chapter 15

After visiting with Megan, still in a coma, and spending time with her sister, who was burnt to a crisp, I wandered over to the police station. Jimmy had sent me a text on some new evidence he had pulled in working a double.

"What's up, Jimmy?" I asked as I walked through the door and chucked my coat on his desk.

"Elliot, I'm glad you're here. I started scanning through public records and found a mountain of information I think you're going to find interesting. Oh, and by the way, all the dead people on this case, other than Victor Martinez, had meth in their systems." Jimmy slapped the lab reports down on the desk.

"Is it all the same brew?" I flipped through the autopsy results that Jimmy had slid across the desk to me.

"It's hard to say, but as you know, meth isn't exactly a big drug in Rhode Island. So take it for what it is." Jimmy took off his glasses and rubbed his eyes. They were bloodshot from having stared at his computer monitor for the past six hours.

I sat down with Jimmy and we started double-teaming the pile of research that had consumed any and all open space that was left in the lab.

"So you're thinking all our stiffs are connected in some way?" I asked.

"They have to be. There's just way too much coincidental information lying here in front of us. It's either that or all the stiffs who were murdered in the past few days were buying drugs from the same house."

"No, I think you're right. There's definitely a pattern here, but why? So what? They're all dopeheads. Why is this guy killing them?"

"I don't know. Maybe these guys were stepping onto someone else's turf."

Jimmy's speculation of gangs selling drugs on the wrong side of the street slapped me in the face like an angry prom date. "You might just be onto something, Jimmy. Who owns the house that was blown to splinters?" I had a quick idea about the case we were building brick by brick.

"I don't know, but I can find out."

"Why, what are you thinking?" Sean strolled through the door and sat down with us, ready to work.

I threw out my impulsive and crazy speculation to my brother officers. "All right, listen. It's a long shot, but what if it's not drug competition? What if VBG Properties is trying to clean up the streets to hold onto property values in the city?"

Sean pursed his lips and mulled it over for a moment. "You know what? Anything is possible. That's actually an interesting angle. I never would've thought of it. Money can make people do crazy shit."

I nodded. "Maybe, just for shits and giggles, we should look into similar crimes from other departments down the East Coast, in cities where VBG has similar interests."

Jimmy called Sean and me over to his computer screen. "Check this out. The meth house—or I should say the property the meth house was on—is owned by JJ&H Properties, LLC. Now give me a second to see who the owner of this LLC is . . . Come on, these computers suck! They are so friggin' slow!" Jimmy threw his hands up in frustration. He was working on black coffee and no sleep. "Ah, here we go. Mr. Eddie Gomez. And what a surprise, he owns fifty-five other rental houses in Providence." Jimmy conveyed the information with a big smile, like we were possibly onto something.

"That's good," I said. "That's real good. Now we have someone to watch other than the Whitmores. Let's print out a list of all the JJ&H properties in the city. Then we'll pull some comparisons with what we have on VBG in those same areas."

"No problem. I'll work on that and print them out now." Jimmy, always hungry for a challenge, pounded the keys and zipped through the records.

"Check on Gomez, too." I said to Sean. "That punk might just be next in line to get whacked."

After giving the two guys—who'd had much more time on the job than I—some work to do, I sat down and raked through the piles, trying to find as much as I could on all the characters who'd had a part in this case and had disrupted the henhouse.

~~~

"Thank you," Grace said.

Steve shut the door to the cab that was parked in their circular driveway, waiting to take them to the airport. The cabby looked in the rearview mirror and asked if they were all set to get rolling. Steve nodded to the driver, who threw the car in gear and pulled away from the beautiful house and breathtaking grounds.

Grace looked out the window as they left their bittersweet getaway behind once again. The cab cruised down the long driveway, passing the old black oak where Steve and Blake had carved their platoon numbers into the bark on the backside. Next they passed by the patch of silver birch trees on the west side, where she remembered Steve telling her for the very first time that he loved her.

The driver slowed down as they approached the gates, roughly a quarter of a mile away from the house. As the cab slowly passed through the gate and approached the road, Grace looked beyond the enormous stone pillars and into the past, remembering when she was a young girl of about thirteen or fourteen years old.

~~~

Grace and a friend from school were walking down the driveway, talking about what boys were cute, and wandered off down to the big wrought iron exit. A man driving along spotted the two young girls alone at the end of the driveway. He stopped and parked his car along the grass mound outside the gated entrance.

Grace saw him get out of his car and walk up to them. That's when he tried to coerce them to come with him.

"Get in the car and come for a drive," he said. "Come on, it'll be fun."

One thing the man and the girls hadn't seen was Grace's seventeen-year-old brother, Blake, who was watching them from the wood line of the property, about one hundred feet away, with his lever-action .22 rifle his father had bought him for his birthday. He'd been hunting and plinking cans along the trail he had cut, away from the house and away from his mother, who would nag him when she'd see him with the handsome rifle.

The man grabbed Grace by the arm. *Crack!* A shot went off in the air. He looked over and saw young Blake move out from cover and walk toward them across the lawn, the muzzle of his rifle pointed right at the man.

The predator let go of Grace's arm, and his shaky hand pointed at Blake. "Boy, you put that rifle down, now, you hear?" the man ordered in a soft and twitchy voice.

Blake turned the rifle to the man's car and squeezed the trigger, blowing out the side window, then quickly cycled the action of the Marlin and put the barrel back on the pedophile's face. "Mister, you get the fuck off my property, *now*, or I'll blast you and leave you heels up in a ditch!"

The man realized Blake was in charge and grabbed his free pass. He booked it to his car, not looking back once. The two young girls and Blake watched him nervously grind the gears, peel out on the grass, and disappear down the road at a new land speed record.

"Get up to the house before I tell Mom and Dad," Blake ordered the two girls, with a grin on his face.

They sprinted up the driveway, unaware of the danger they would have been in if Blake hadn't been their guardian angel that day.

~~~

Grace grabbed Steve's hand in the back of the cab as they made a left out of the driveway, where Grace's big brother had saved her life and had left his mark as the man of 17 Shadow Pond Drive.

Chapter 16

"Elliot, come check this out." Sean, who had been dredging through public records for hours, flagged me over with two fingers.

"What'd ya find?"

"Look at this, right here." Sean pointed a third of the way down the screen. "Eighty percent of JJ&H houses have been involved with drug raids, prostitution, and enough domestic calls to build a bridge from here to Europe."

"Drug raids, huh? Does anything filter back to Gomez?"

"Actually, he's pretty clean. He has a couple of priors on him for assault and battery. Let's see . . . Ah, yeah, look right here. Last year he beat up his plasterer with one of the guy's stilts right in the middle of Broadway, in front of two cops drinking their coffee. Another arrest was in 2007. It says here he kicked in the door to one of his apartments on the South Side and slapped around an eighteen-year-old hooker and her roommate, and then threw her down the stairs. I'm sure the list goes on, and I'm sure there's a sleazy lawyer on retainer who's washed a lot of dirty laundry for Mr. Gomez."

"What about VBG? Same type of trouble in their buildings?"

Sean pulled up their history that he had on file. "VBG is a little tougher because it's a much older company. The information that shows up online is mostly recent, and to be honest with you, irrelevant to our case. Without doing serious amounts of digging, and asking favors like Jimmy did, we're at the end of the road with them."

I pointed to the middle of the screen. "What about that?"

Sean clicked the mouse. "The *Providence Journal* featured them in the real estate section a few years ago. That's a picture of Grace and Blake for the article, 'The Fundamentals of Real Estate in the Northeast.' I'm telling you, there's no police record on file for Blake, Grace, or VBG."

"Well, then, I guess we should start looking a little closer at our boy Eddie G. Actually, can you get an address on Eddie for me? I'm gonna run up to see if vice has anything on him. I'll be back."

"I'll see what I can do." Sean got back on the keyboard, pecking at it like a bird eating seed.

I climbed the rear stairwell up to the third floor to pop in on Mark Grandy, a vice cop affiliated with the DEA. Mark and I got along really well because he and I had chewed the same soil over in the Middle East back in '02 and '03.

I knocked on the metal doorjamb to his office and stuck my head in. "Do you have a minute?"

"Hey, Elliot. Come on in." Mark flagged me in, and then he pulled off his reading glasses and put them on his desk. "What's up?"

"Same old shit, different pile, man." I reached across his desk to shake his hand, and sat down across from him.

"Yeah, I know about that pile. Hey, by the way, that was a hell of a shot you made the other day." Mark put out his fist for a bump.

"Yeah, thanks." I skipped all the foreplay and dived straight into the subject that was still fresh in my mind. "Mark, have you had any dealings with Eddie Gomez?"

"Oh yeah, I've had a few run-ins with that greaseball. He's one of these guys that's real smart, though. He never puts his paw prints on anything. We were actively watching those guys that were brutally murdered in the basement the other day, because of the tremendous amounts of product they'd been moving for Gomez this past year."

"Let me guess, you guys were close to a bust, right?"

"How'd you know? Probably another month and we would've had them. Hey, fuck it. At least it was only, like, eight months' worth of work, and we hadn't been following them for two years or something. Then I'd be real pissed." Mark tore open the wrapper to a Hershey's bar he'd pulled out of his desk drawer. "Want a piece?"

I couldn't say no to a Hershey's with Almonds, so I grabbed the end and snapped off half. "Thanks, Mark."

"Any time."

"What about the other dirtbags? Any of their names float across your desk?"

"Oh God, yeah. I've had run-ins with all these dirtbags. The cookers that got blown up the other day were junkies that worked for Gomez and were supporting their own bad habits. The two psychopaths that robbed the bank were high-ranked officers in Gomez's squad. I hear he's pretty pissed about the whole ordeal."

I nodded. "I got Sean Kelley probing around, trying to find out where Eddie lives. Starting tomorrow, I'm going to start keeping tabs on this maggot Gomez, if that's okay by you."

"I can save you guys some time on that. He lives in Barrington out on Rumstick Point. Big fuckin' house, right on the main drag. You can't miss it." Mark grabbed a yellow Post-it and wrote down the address from the file he'd pulled.

I left his office and headed back to the stairwell, where I ran into Miranda Kemp, a patrolwoman who I'd gone through the academy with. We'd also dated for about a year.

"Hi, Elliot. How are you?" Miranda seduced me with her lip movements. She cocked her hips deep to the right as she put her hands on her gun belt.

"I'm doing all right. It's been kind of tough with Megan in the hospital. It just makes everything that much harder, you know?"

Miranda appeased me with a sad face. "What if I come over tonight and keep you warm?" She grabbed my tie and tugged on it. Her smile and pouty lips would break most men.

"I'm flattered, but you know I can't do that, Miranda. I'm engaged to be married." I started to sweat, overheating with the lust that had wrapped itself around my neck.

"Sure you can," Miranda whispered in my ear. "You're not even trying. I miss what's under this shirt." She slid her hand from my chest to below my beltline, and flooded my senses with a peach aroma that drove me crazy.

"I'm sorry. I just can't." I backed up, knowing that avenue couldn't be traveled again.

She let go of my tie, and then ironed it out with her hand. "You know my number. If you change your mind, use it." She brushed me on her way past and kept my full attention while swaying out of sight, leaving me with visual memories that threatened to send me to the locker room for a cold shower.

I looked around to see how many people had seen that little clip. In this place, it could turn into that we were having sex against the candy machine. It seemed as if I was in the clear, so I grabbed a couple of snacks from the half-empty vending machine and a coffee from the break room before heading down to see what Sean had found.

Major Sullivan called to me from his office as I walked by. "Elliot, hold on."

"Hey, Major. What's up?"

"IID wants you to take a couple days off with pay for stress relief."

"Come on, you know—"

"I know." Sullivan cut me off mid-complaint. "Listen, this day's almost over." He peeked at his stainless diving-style watch. "Take tomorrow off, and there's your two days. Boom, it goes away. They're happy. No big deal."

"Yeah, of course, Major. Sure." I relented, not wanting to bitch and cry and fill up the major's bowl more than it already was.

"Good. Now enjoy your time off."

I turned to leave.

"Elliot," he said, stopping me in my tracks.

I peeked my head back in, holding onto the jamb of his door. "Yeah?"

"The day off tomorrow... Doesn't mean you can't do some snooping from home. But you didn't hear that from me." Sullivan smiled and nodded once, then picked up the phone on his desk that had started to ring.

I made my way back to Sean, feeling a great sense of relief that Internal Affairs wasn't going after my jugular.

"He lives in Barrington." I filled Sean in on Eddie's location and sat down.

"Yeah, I know. Oh man, peanut M&M's and a Hershey's with Almonds, my favorites."

I tossed the bag and bar onto his desk and watched him tear into the colorful candy pieces.

"Rumstick Point in the a.m.?" he said, munching away on the chocolate.

Watching Sean enjoy the snack I'd brought him gave me a shot of gusto. "Yeah. We'll leave here first thing, eight o'clock sharp."

I decided to get out of the department for the day and left Sean to his research. I needed to stay under the radar for my so-called two-day vacation.

Chapter 17

Grace and Steve were somewhere over the Carolinas on their flight back to Rhode Island. Steve looked over at Grace, conked out from the Valium she'd washed down with her Seven and Seven. He rolled the last sip of scotch around in his glass and peered out the small side window into the early dusk, gazing at the marker light somewhere toward the end of the wing.

He found himself thinking back to his childhood, to when he was living with his uncle up in the mountains of Vermont.

~~~

"Come on, boy. Wake your ass up! You're twelve years old now. What are you going to do if the Commies invade this country?"

Steve, still half asleep, looked up at his uncle, a decorated Korean War vet, who was dressed in military fatigues and armed with a Colt 1911 on his side.

"You'd better be downstairs and ready to go in two minutes," Steve's uncle, John Thomas, said sternly. Then he stomped out and slammed the door behind him.

Steve got up and looked at his wristwatch. A patrolman had given it to him along with his parents' personal belongings on the night of their deadly automobile accident. His watch read just three thirty in the morning, but he dared not disobey his uncle, for fear that he'd catch himself a beating.

He put the oversized watch, which was still too big for him to wear, back on his nightstand, and got dressed. He booked it down to the kitchen in less than two minutes, and then he tied his boots, gobbled down a dry piece of toast, and drank a glass of water on the way out.

Steve patted Reggie, their hound dog, on the shoulder and walked out into the lonely, frigid November air, shutting the front door behind him. Smoke puffed out of the bent tailpipe of the old green Ford pickup while Uncle John finished scraping frost off the front and side windows. Steve hopped in and sat on the bench seat, which felt like a cold piece of granite against his ass, and stared out the open door down the driveway.

He envisioned that his mom and dad would come rolling up in their black sedan and take young Steve into their arms. He often stared into space with the same dream, though he knew it would never come true.

Uncle John threw the scraper onto the seat and climbed into the cold cab of the truck, closed his door, and told Steve to do the same. The obsessive-compulsive vet shifted into first on the column and took off down the long and winding driveway. "I know you probably think I'm a prick, but someday you'll thank me when you're alive and the people that surround you can't get out of their own way. Don't think for a minute that someone's going to wipe your ass for you when you're tits deep in war, boy! That's a fact!" Uncle John pumped the clutch and shifted the three-on-the-tree into third as he came barrel-assing out of the driveway and onto the main road.

Cigarette smoke and conversation filled up the cab of the truck. Steve hopped around on the seat as they cut down old logging roads and out into the middle of nowhere. He had grown up in a neighborhood with kids and stickball games. Now it took thirty minutes to get to any type of civilization.

"Woah!" Steve exclaimed as the truck braked with no warning and slid sideways. He skated off the hard, slippery seat, nearly smashing his head against the dashboard in the process.

Uncle John reached over and opened Steve's door. "All right, we're about five miles from home. Here's your hunting knife. Now stay out of sight. I expect to see you home for breakfast." He nudged Steve out of the cab and took off up the road, leaving the boy in a cloud of exhaust.

Steve watched the taillights disappear into the mysterious and terrifying early morning blackness. He understood what his uncle's intentions were, but hated living with him and wished things were different. Fortunately, young Steve Krasson always paid attention to what he was told and was a very visual person. He knew every left and right his uncle had made on the hell ride that had dropped him off into the arms of independence and manhood.

Steve looked up periodically to read the stars as he sprinted along the side of the bumpy dirt road. He sniffled and wiped his nose, which ran like a faucet onto his face. After a few turns and roughly an hour on his feet, Steve looked up to the tower that stood on top of the highest peak, its red and white marker lights warning planes that land was near.

Out of the blue, he heard a massive commotion in the woods, like a freight train moving alongside him. Steve put on the brakes and stood silently as the noise got louder and eventually revealed its identity by jumping out onto the road. He froze in total fear, his nose leaking and upper lip quivering as he faced a huge problem.

The young man's heavy breath poured out into the frigid air as four mangy dogs growled at him, showing off their sharp teeth and letting Steve know they meant business. He pulled his blade out of his back pocket and squared off with the pack of wild dogs, which were capable of ending his life in about the same time it had taken him to put on his boots. He knew that he couldn't back down or show them he was scared, or he'd be done.

The feral dogs formed a circle around Steve. Then the leader of the pack sprang through the air and knocked him to the ground. The 80-pound killer mutt wasted no time. He lunged at Steve, bit into his ear and cheekbone, and awakened young Mr. Krasson's killer instinct.

Steve's eyes rolled back, and his fear disappeared. The pain of the bite and his built-up anger at the whole situation drove him to see red, and he exploded. Gripping the handle of his knife with everything he had, he slashed at the yellow-eyed monster, cutting him across the neck and collarbone. Steve had caught the bully off guard. Surprised and able to sense that the boy was willing to go the distance, the nasty beast jumped up with a yelp, announcing to his crew to leave this one alone.

The pack galloped away, back into the forest and out of his sight, leaving Steve bloody and his head throbbing. But he also felt powerful knowing he hadn't backed down and had won his first fight.

~~~

"Excuse me, Mr. Whitmore. Would you like another drink, sir?" The onboard flight attendant pulled Steve out of his memories and back to his empty glass, which he handed over for a refill.

He touched his ear and the past flooded his emotions. He wondered why he'd had to be with his uncle in the first place. Steve forced himself to let go of the past, as he'd learned to, and took the refill that the attendant handed him.

Steve looked down at the single malt and took a sip. He reached down and grabbed the handle of the double-edged dagger tucked away under his coat. His next victim was in sight.

Chapter 18

I took a spin to the lower end of North Main Street to visit my friend Lenny, who owned a little flower shop, and to get a change of scenery. I had lived a block and a half away from the shop when I first moved into the city after leaving the Corps.

At that time, trying to get on the force and into the academy, I was still running a lot, and I'd pass by his generational legacy almost every day. Lenny and I became very good friends. "Good morning" and "Hello" turned into "Did you catch the game last night?" and "How about those taxes." It didn't take long before I was sitting in front of the shop with Lenny, smoking cigars and sharing our thoughts on life while watching women jog by. We'd spent some stellar nights overlooking the city as all the worker bees flew home and everything wound back down to a normal pulse.

"Lenny, what's up, man?" I announced as I walked in.

"Hey, Elliot. How's Megan? I left a message on your voice mail." Lenny walked over to me with true concern on his face and gave me a big hug.

"I know you did, and I appreciate it. I'm sorry I haven't gotten back to you. It's just been crazy."

"Come on, let's sit in the garden."

"I'd love to, Len, but I'm going over to visit Megan. I was hoping you could put together one of your house arrangements for me."

"Say no more. It will be ready in ten minutes, my friend." Without hesitation, he started to gather all of the elements he needed.

Whenever I'd visit Lenny or stop by for the occasional present to tell Meg "I love you" or "I'm sorry," I'd always check out the family photo collage that covered one wall made from old barn board and shingles. The place definitely had a lot of character. Handmade trinkets had been added through the years by Lenny's family, and of course there were a few very memorable pictures of the two of us—some at the store on days like those mentioned earlier and some at local bars and charity events around the city.

I'd learned so much about the city and its past from Lenny's family, who were Providence natives. Primo, his grandfather, who stood five foot four and was ninety-two years old, lived two doors down from the shop and would walk over and join us in much of our storefront dialogue. Primo had opened the shop in 1938 with his wife, Anna, and his late brother Angelo.

He'd share memories that were layered on top of each other like a tall wedding cake. Primo had taken us on private tours through the paths of his past, where hidden secrets hung from lampposts and unsolved mysteries still lingered that had created enough tears to burn gullies into the walls and thin out the guts of the city. Some of those very stories had seared certain instincts into me from the other side of what the law saw and heard.

"Here you go, Elliot," Lenny said, recapturing my attention. "How's this?"

"Oh man, that's perfect."

I paid for the flowers, even though Lenny tried to give them to me for free. We made some loose plans to get together as I made my way out the door and back into the mix.

~~~

I made it to the hospital and up to Megan's private room, and placed the flowers on the table across from her bed, next to an arrangement from my parents. I gave Denise a hug and pulled up a chair beside the bed. My phone started going off as soon as I sat down. I looked at the screen and saw that it was my buddy Ken Sast, from the airport.

I knew I had to answer. "Hey, Ken. What's up?"

"Hey, Elliot. They're in flight, but they're going to land in fifteen minutes. I'm sorry, man. My guy was tied up on a few different things and just let me know."

"I'll be there." I ended the call and kissed Megan on her forehead. On my way to the door, I gently squeezed her sister's shoulder as I passed. "Call me if you need me, sis."

I sprinted as fast as I could to my car, jumped into my seat, flipped on the lights, and headed off, doing what I did best: breaking the speed limit. I cut through side streets and wove up and down one-ways and across a vacant lot to grab quick access to the highway. I rolled down the on-ramp, pedal to the floor, and cut across three lanes like a wild banshee carving it up through a cowboy-filled canyon on his best horse.

I shot up the high-speed lane, watching the cars in front of me shed across the pavement and over the crown of the road like a big wave. The motorists moved as far away as they could from the enormous bullet that lit up the entire roadway with red and blue strobes. I stormed by the Jersey barrier, solid and straight and just feet from my window, at speeds of over 120.

I pulled up to the main entrance at T. F. Green and parked in the same spot as before. With just a couple of minutes to spare, Ken met me at the door and brought me to the terminal where my friends would be walking in.

I sat down and grabbed a newspaper off the seat next to me, and casually flipped through it while I waited. I got a text from Ken, who was up in the control tower, giving me a heads-up that they were walking in. I slipped the phone in my pocket and camouflaged my mug with the business section. Some guy wearing a cowboy hat and standing in front of his new steakhouse in East Greenwich stared back at me from its pages.

I didn't want to be seen, but I didn't want to lose them, either, so I slowly lowered the paper, exposing my eyes to the people getting off the escalator on the second floor. An eerie feeling drove right through me and down my back, lifting the hairs on my neck. I ignored my phone that was vibrating nonstop in my pocket.

"Hello, Detective Frantallo," a voice said from behind me on my right side.

I closed the paper, put it back on the seat beside me, and turned my head to meet the man behind the voice that had just flipped on the lights and revealed my cover.   I found myself eye to eye with the man who had allowed Grace to board the luxury jet ahead of him, a tough and rugged man with a solid broad frame and a head of thick salt-and-pepper hair. He was clean-shaven, unlike the other day, and his eyes told me he was used to running the show.

I played the dumb game. "Do I know you?" I asked, my thoughts fumbling around to make sense of what was happening. He had caught me off guard.

He played the dumb game back, serving overhand. "Blake Whitmore." He gave me a powerful look, then slid on his tinted frames, covering his eyes that were like pools of water at the bottom of an abandoned well. "I just wanted to come over and thank you for cleaning up the streets around here, Detective. I was fortunate enough to catch the news report, and learned that Providence has a new hero."

"Tell that to Internal Affairs."

"Forget about them. It's time someone stepped up to the plate and put on their vigilante cap."

"Yeah, I don't know about vigilante, but that fucking asshole deserved to die." I tried to validate my kill as an officer of the law to my new acquaintance.

"You don't have to be on the defensive with me, Detective. I'm glad you did what you did. Anyone with brains, I'm pretty sure, feels the same way." Blake laughed as he spoke to me, happy with the job I'd done. "You can't worry about the idiots who can't think their way past the big pile of cow shit that fell off the back of the truck in front of them. Come on, I'm sure every single person on your force would've given you the order to hollow out the back of that maggot's head if they hadn't had protocol and procedure to follow. Let's face it, everyone's afraid to step out of line, even if it means doing the right thing."

Blake had scratched my itch that I hadn't been able to reach. But I couldn't let this silver-tongued bastard kiss my ear and slip into my psyche.

"I don't know about that," I said. "But I really don't give a shit, because I saved two innocent people by ending his miserable existence."

"Once again, Detective, you don't have to sell me on what you did." Blake got up and signaled a curve ball salute off the corner of his eyebrow, and then he turned and began to walk away.

"Blake, wait!" I stood up, not wanting him to leave just yet. "Do you know a man by the name of Steve Krasson?" I had to hit him with the best shot I had before he flew away on me again.

"I did, Detective. He was a friend from the war. Why?"

"We kind of tripped over him in this investigation we have going on."

Blake stood with his back facing me. "Then you know he's dead, right? The gators were the last ones to talk to him before they had him for dinner."

I sprinted over between him and Grace, who was waiting at the exit of the terminal, holding her carry-on and looking rather impatient. "I just want to know one more thing."

"Yeah, sure. Go ahead."

"Are you back in Rhode Island on business or pleasure?" I asked, knowing that I was pushing my luck. It was worth the risk for the chance to read his facial expression for the real answer.

"Let's just say it's a little bit of both, Mr. Frantallo." Blake Whitmore answered the question with not one pinched nerve, unconcerned and calm, and with as much emotion as bark on a maple tree. "I'm sorry, Detective, but we really have to go." He excused himself and walked out of the terminal with Grace.

Ken walked up to me and put his hand on my shoulder. "I'm sorry, man. I was trying to text you to let you know that he'd sat right behind you."

"Don't worry about it, Ken. This guy plays on a much different field than the people we're used to playing against."

"Did you get anything you wanted?"

"Not quite, man, but thanks for all your help. If you ever need anything, make sure you call me." I shook hands with Ken and left the airport, fighting a headache from all the voices that were scraping the walls of my brain.

I decided to call it a day, so I drove home. I glanced over at Jack's house as I got out of my car, and through the side window saw Janice with him in the kitchen. Funny how things can change in the snap of a finger.

I shut and locked the front door behind me, and dropped a trail of clothes on the floor as I walked to my bed and collapsed facedown. I rolled onto my back and stared at the ceiling, trying to add up the information on this case like an accountant crunching numbers at tax time.

My eyes felt heavy as my mind closed down. Thinking about the day's events had me looking ahead to what the next day would bring and searching for an answer to make sense of why it felt as if I was chasing my tail.

Chapter 19

Steve Krasson lay on his back a couple miles away from Elliot's front door, trying to catch his breath. Grace, sticky with drying sweat, drew on his chest with her finger, wondering if this Providence detective was coming a little too close.

"Once I take out Eddie Gomez," Steve said, "we'll gain control of at least fifty percent of his properties. Who knows . . . in this economy, maybe all of them."

Grace stopped doodling and placed her hand down flat on his broad chest. "Do you think we should wait?"

"Why, because of our detective friend? Please, he can circle around me all he wants, but he will never bite."

Steve's eyes fixed on the red and orange colors that crawled across the ceiling, projected from the lava lamp that sat on a reproduction Shaker table he and Grace had purchased in Little Compton from a local furniture maker.

~~~

Steve stares into the flames of napalm that spread across the jungle and roll up on both North Vietnamese and American troops. Watching from a distance through his scope, he can see the outlines of bodies as they are consumed by the fire and collapse, totally helpless. Sweat rises up and covers his body as he lies still in a patch of bamboo. He starts to shake and moan while watching both sides fry in a big oven that sends their souls up to the clouds in smoke.

~~~

Steve opened his eyes as his body jolted, waking up Grace. They were both covered in sweat from his nightmare. He got up and went to the bathroom to rinse his face with cold water. He looked in the mirror as he shut off the faucet, knowing that nothing lasted forever. He dried himself off and walked into the den.

Steve made his way to the backside of the room, near the couch, and felt along the floor-to-ceiling raised cherry paneling. He opened a secret door that was totally invisible to anyone but him and Grace. The private walk-in safe that Grace's parents had used to tuck away their cash was still used by Steve, but for different reasons. He entered the combination to unlock the big chrome wheel, turned it clockwise, and pushed the door open.

Steve Krasson walked into the steel room that was outfitted with dehumidified, conditioned air and hit a switch to turn on the light. As the fluorescent lights warmed up, the walls started to take shape, revealing rifles and handguns that each had their own special spot. The outline of Steve's collection began to grow the brighter the secret room became.

Once it was bright as day, the weapons showed off their separate traits that made each of them unique. Steve walked over and picked up his favorite, an all-black heavy-barrel .338 Lapua, and got reacquainted with his old friend in preparation for their next kill.

Grace peeked her head in. "You know, it's two thirty in the morning. Are you all right?"

"I'm fine. Just give me a few minutes, okay?"

"Of course, Steve."

He held up the rifle, pulled it in tight, and looked through the clear protective lens covers of the scope. "Good-bye, Gomez." Steve tapped the trigger, seeing the shot and kill in his mind.

~~~

I walk through a door into one of the conference rooms at the station, where Blake sits at a table all alone. I tread lightly across the floor to the lone chair across from him, pull it out, and sit down, looking at him, ready to ask all my questions about what he knows.

I question him while looking straight into his big round black eyes. "Blake, are you back in Rhode Island for business or pleasure?"

He pulls himself in closer. "You already asked me that question."

"You're right. I'm sorry." I look around, not prepared to go on. My mind has gone blank.

Megan, dressed in her hospital johnny, comes to the table with two bowls of cereal and places them in front of us.

"When did you get out of the hospital?" I ask, stunned.

"I'm just visiting, Elliot. I can't stay." She turns and walks back through a black door in the corner of the room.

I look back at Blake and the cereal bowls Megan left in front of us. I hear a bang and look over to see the door she disappeared through fall off the wall, exposing a bush that's covered with bees' nests. I walk over to the bush. Swarms of hornets, yellow jackets, and wasps are everywhere.

"This is definitely business." Blake yanks me back to my seat, then looks away from me as if he's hiding something.

"Blake, turn around so I can see you." His odd behavior makes me a little nervous. *"Look at me, Blake!"* I grab for my sidearm. It's not in my holster.

Blake starts to turn his head toward me. My entire body tenses up, cold like an icicle, unable to move a muscle. He opens his mouth, releasing a swarm of bees that fly by me like bullets, and then all of his teeth start falling out onto the table and scatter everywhere. He has this look on his face that makes me feel as if I'm responsible.

I start sweeping up the piles of teeth into a tactical desert boot in my left hand. When I sweep the last of the teeth off the table, I look into the boot. It's empty. *"Where did all the teeth go?"* I turn back to Blake and show him the empty boot.

He smiles and turns to the door. *"Megan's coming back."*

I look to the door Megan walked out of earlier and find myself flying through the empty door as if I were thrown. I look around and grab the wheel of the car that I'm buckled into and sail down the highway at top speed, completely out of control.

The vehicle feels as if it's floating on rough waters as it takes me on this hell ride. I just keep going faster and faster as the road narrows down to one lane. The force pushes against my chest, smashing me back into my seat as if I'm on a jet. The trees whip by just inches from my touch, and the velocity triggers my heart to start pounding as it climbs at a steady pace that consumes my throat.

I'm finding it hard to breathe and don't recognize where I am, or even the car that I am driving, but I know if I don't find a way to stop this vortex, I'll be in big trouble. I try stepping on the brake that I immediately realize doesn't exist. I look down to see my foot buried in a bunch of vines that are growing up my leg. I can't pull myself free.

I try to turn the steering wheel, but it just spins around in circles like a game of roulette. I look through the windshield at a garbage truck parked up ahead that has something spray-painted in orange on the side of it.

I'm frozen in my seat, totally incapable of controlling this runaway caboose. I notice something or someone out of the corner of my eye and glance over to inspect the passenger's seat, which was empty the last time I looked. Victor Martinez is strapped in and smoking a cigarette, staring like a zombie out past the hood of the vehicle.

I train my focus back on the death ride that's taking me to who knows where, and the windshield starts getting sprayed with bullets. I grip the steering wheel, praying that I don't get shot by the barrage of lead that is turning the glass into Swiss cheese.

I turn to Martinez and ask him if he can make out the words on the side of the trash truck. "Martinez, what does it say? Answer me, God damn it!"

Martinez doesn't answer me. I scream his name as loud as I can, banging and pulling on the steering wheel in a fit of rage. He slowly turns in my direction, responding to my outburst, and stares at me with distant eyes that are runny and wet. They drip down his face onto the dashboard, fill up the instrument panel, and overflow onto me.

My attention homes in on the wetness that is coming out of his alabaster eyeballs and is now pouring from his ears. Martinez opens his slimy black mouth and turns into Jack Pollenso, right before my very eyes.

"Jack, what's on the side of the truck?" I ask urgently.

I feel the wind rush through my hair and perilous electricity run through my body. I brace myself while the nose of the vehicle folds under the thick steel of the garbage truck.

"I can't crash today," I spit out. "I need to find Eddie Gomez! Where's Blake?"

I feel death tugging at my feet and pulling me down through the fire wall. The steel of the truck is only inches from collapsing the windshield that Jack and I eyeball with unbroken terror.

~~~

I heard birds singing and looked up into the sky, and then I sprang out of bed like a rabbit from that crazy dream, my heart pumping overtime. I looked around my room while I panted profusely, still not acclimated to what was or was not real. I leaned on my bureau as I focused myself back into reality.

I got dressed and ran through my bizarre dream, trying to remember why I'd been interrogating Blake down at headquarters, but my memory kept getting covered with clouds, making it impossible to remember much about what had happened.

I got into my car and backed out into the street, and tooted the horn to Jack. He wasn't outside again, so I drove off.

Chapter 20

My phone rang as I was thinking about trading places with some college kids that I'd passed by on the way to work.

"Hello?" I answered.

"Morning, Elliot," Sean said. "I'm out on the Fire side."

"I'll be there in two minutes. I'm on the overpass now."

I pulled up to the south side of the station, where Sean stood waiting in the lot nearest to the overhead doors where the fire trucks parked. He got in, handed me a coffee, and shut his door.

He brought out something in foil and began to unwrap it. "Want a piece of banana bread?"

"Absolutely." I grabbed a piece from the foil. A bite of the moist homemade treat and the smell of the hot coffee in my cup holder woke my senses, putting me at 100 percent and ready to go.

I grabbed another piece off the half loaf that Sean had offered to me and looked out the window, wondering what my dream was all about and realizing how my dreams had changed since all this shit started.

Sean looked over at me. "Are you all right, man?"

"Yeah, I'm fine. Who made this, your mom?" I took the last bite of my breakfast and tried to move away from my overloaded brain.

"Yeah, I stopped by there last night, and she gave me the loaf. She made, like, three of them."

We ran down 195 East, heading to Barrington—Rumstick Point, to be exact. Rumstick Point was a very exclusive area. If Eddie G. lived there, he had either inherited a boatload of money, had a big education that filled his pockets, which I doubted, or he was up to no good.

"Pull out that picture of Eddie again." I looked at the mug shot that Sean handed me and saw a clean-cut, metrosexual middle-aged man who poured out attitude.

We passed by a brackish channel of water and the Barrington public high school, as well as a town cop parked in the exit of the bank lot, taking radar, as we entered into the quiet community. We followed Sean's GPS to Eddie's address, which was four-tenths of a mile and one right turn from our location.

We gawked out the windows at the beautiful homes full of character and charm, surrounded by vine-covered stone walls and beautiful green lawns. The small computerized map alerted us that we had arrived, so we pulled off to the side and stopped the car where the number on the mailbox coincided with the file that Sean held in his hands.

We both looked at each other, eyebrows raised in surprise, and then turned back for a second look at the SOLD sign that sat on the front lawn.

Sean held his forehead and squeezed his eyes shut. "Oh, what the fuck!"

"We have to find where this motherfucker is!" I shouted.

"How the hell are we going to find that out today?"

I grabbed my phone and dialed the listing agent's number off the sign.

"Now what are you doing?" Sean grinned and shook his head.

"Good morning!" the chipper voice on the other end of the line sang out. "Blue Skies Realty, this is Barbara. How may I help you?"

"Good morning, Barbara. My name is Gregg Koenig, and I was wondering if I could speak with"—I quickly read the name from the SOLD sign—"Ned Francis, please."

"Ned won't be in for another half hour. Would you like his voice mail?"

"That would be great, Barbara. But first, could you tell me who purchased this lovely home that I have missed out on?"

"What's the address, Mr. Koenig?"

"It's 520 Spruce Hill."

"Let me see . . . Oh, that's right. Bill and Gail Harkam purchased 520 Spruce Hill."

"Those lucky dogs. I'll tell ya, some people . . . Oh well. I'll take Ned's voice mail now."

"Of course, I'll put you right in, Mr. Koenig. You have a nice day."

Ned's voice mail sounded off before I could reply. "Here, leave a message with a callback number," I whispered to Sean as I handed over my cell.

"Hi Ned, this is Gregg Koenig. I'm interested in setting up a meeting to look at some of your listings. Please call me back." Sean left my number and hung up.

We drove in circles for a while after grabbing some tall iced coffees and a peek at the ocean to burn some time.

I looked at my recent calls, and at what time I had called the realty company. "It's been an hour. I can't wait anymore." I dialed again.

"Good morning! Blue Skies Realty, this is Barbara. How may I help you?"

"Good morning, Barbara. Is Ned in, please?" I grabbed my tie and got into character while Sean watched me with wide eyes and shook his head.

"May I ask who's calling?"

"It's Bill Harkam."

"Oh, of course, Mr. Harkam, let me transfer you."

I looked over at Sean, grinning, and gave him a thumbs-up.

"Good morning, Ned speaking."

"Ned, Bill Harkam," I said.

"Bill, how are you? Have you and the missus started to move in yet?"

"Actually, Gail and I went over to take some measurements yesterday, and I just wanted to let you know how happy we are with the house."

"Well, thank you, Bill. I try my best."

"Ned, Gail and I would like to send Eddie a gift certificate to show him our appreciation for the fine job he did cleaning up."

Sean stifled a chuckle and slugged me in the arm, impressed by my idea.

Ned hesitated for a few seconds. "Sure, I can't see the harm in that. Do you have something to write with?"

"I'm all set. Give it to me."

Sean waited with pen and pad in hand as I switched the call to speaker.

"His new address is 171 Fort Wetherill Road, Jamestown."

"Oh, that's wonderful, Ned. My sister will be calling you soon. She's looking into a summer house in the area." I threw Ned a white lie, filling up his trunk with enough bullshit to take his mind off the already twisted story I had going on.

"Okay, tell her to ask for . . ."

"Ned, I'm sorry to cut you off, but Gail's trying to call me on the other line. Have a good day." I hung up, putting an abrupt end to the fabrication.

Sean shook his head. "You're something else."

A sense of déjà vu ran through my veins as I saw Sean scratch his ear. My dream of Martinez popped into my head, along with a vision of Blake's teeth falling out. "Shit!"

"What's wrong?" Sean asked.

"Blake's ear. I forgot to look at his ear at the airport yesterday. God damn it!"

We headed down Route 24 toward Newport to swing in for an

unannounced visit on the quiet island of Jamestown and check out Eddie's new pad.

Chapter 21

Stave Krasson crouched his way through some brush and found himself stepping out into a small clearing at the edge of a cliff. The tiny opening consisted of long blades of dry grass and a small group of cedar trees growing out of the cracks in the ledge, pointing toward the ocean that crashed against the bottom of the cliff face roughly a hundred feet below.

He had been running around the old fort's acreage all morning, familiarizing himself with the rough, overgrown land that held on to several underground army bunkers, now covered with layers of graffiti. The old war fort, owned by the state, abutted Eddie Gomez's new purchase.

Steve slid and slithered his way quietly across to the spot he'd chosen as his viewing post. He sat down, opened up his canteen, and quenched his thirst while leaning against the base of a small scrub pine. He grabbed the spotting scope from his backpack and pulled a piece of Grace's panty hose around the front of the lens to reduce glare.

He looked through the oversized optical and figured he was sitting back around 450 yards. Steve sized up Eddie's property in its entirety, admiring the grounds while he did so.

Steve swept every inch of the property through his scope before moving it to look inside the house through a huge rear window. The back door suddenly opened, and two large dogs came barreling out and ran full speed until they reached the end of the property.

Steve watched the two Akitas as they leaned on the fence and barked into the woods at some wild turkeys carving their way through the underbrush behind the fence, out of reach of the curious dogs. He heard someone yelling very faintly in the distance and scanned back to the house. A man who Steve knew was not Eddie G. called out to the aggressive and powerful dogs as he walked out toward them, whistling and clapping his hands together. The dogs gave him their full attention and bolted across the back lawn toward him and into the house.

Steve followed the two hounds and the young man with his scope. He was in his late twenties, clean-cut, and dressed as if he was about to walk the runway. The dogs and the man walked past a series of large windows and met up with Steve's primary target: the one and only Eddie Gomez.

Steve held focus on the room as the dogs jumped on Eddie. To his surprise, so did the young man. He blinked to adjust his view and took another look, pulling his focus back to the two men who had started to kiss each other passionately.

A young woman wearing a thong bikini caught Steve's attention as she walked into the room and interrupted the two men. To Steve's surprise, she joined them in the tongue twist, then slid down their bodies and started satisfying both men as they focused their attention back on each other. It didn't take long before the threesome ended up in one big ball, taking turns on each other in many different formations and positions.

Steve put down the scope, confused by the freak show he had just watched for free. He spotted something off in the distance and raised his scope again. A white, four-door, late-model BMW turned onto the property and sat waiting at the front gate. Steve alternated glances between the entrance to the property and Eddie G., who buzzed them in, then hurriedly zipped his fly and buckled his belt.

The bright white sedan, trimmed in chrome with oversized wheels to match, pulled up the driveway as the gate rolled back across the entrance, closing the guests in. The car pulled up to the front landing, and two sharply dressed men Steve had seen before stepped out of the hundred-thousand-dollar ride and onto the red-and-tan paver driveway worth more than double that price tag.

They approached the front door, each carrying a briefcase, and the young woman who had just been tossed around like a pancake in the threesome opened the large, modernistic twin doors, her bare double-D silicone missiles staring them straight in the face. She hugged and kissed the two of them as they passed by her and went straight to Eddie.

Steve watched as Eddie and his boy toy fanned through stacks of money from the briefcases the men had carried in. Meanwhile, Eddie's associates cut into a mountain of coke that sat on the glass table in front of them. They tested the product, snorting up while the half-naked bimbo pranced around the four johns, getting off on the constant attention.

The guests drooled over her body as she lowered her lime-green thong to around her knees, bent over in front of them, and hit a big line they had cut for her. She stepped out of her thong, and the now stark-naked woman began dancing around and giving the guests very elaborate X-rated lap dances.

A helicopter passed by and broke Steve's concentration. His head jerked to the left, pulling him away from the party. The helicopter was heading east toward Newport at a good clip and riding lower than a usual commercial chopper would. Steve stared at the local news chopper as it swooped down, hugging the contour of the cliffs, and drifted across the ocean surface.

~~~

Steve Krasson's twisted-up subconscious drowns out the distinct sound of Huey blades chopping through the air. He sees Blake right in front of him, lying in the wide-open gut of the HU-1 that had brought them together that day. A couple more guys hop on, filling the Huey, and signal to Steve that the landing zone is becoming very hot.

The chopper starts to lift off the ground. Blake yells to Steve, but the powerful army-green chopper pulls up with such deafening and turbulent mayhem that his words go unheard, and Steve has to fight to hold on. Steve stands on the landing gear, and Blake grabs fistfuls of his shirt when the ride gets a bit sideways and bumpy. The NVA are doing everything in their power to shoot the bird out of the sky.

Steve manages to pull himself into the Huey with Blake and the others. "What did you yell to me?" he shouts to Blake.

"Seventeen Shadow Pond Drive, De Funiak Springs, Florida. That's my address, so you know how to find me."

Steve's new friend stares off into the crystal-blue sky as they fly away from a situation that, like so many others, could have been the end.

~~~

Steve pulled out of his midmorning flashback as the colorful copter passed over the shores across the bay, becoming one solid color that blended in with the horizon and architecture of historical Newport. He put the scope back up to his eye only to see Eddie walking away from him, down the hallway and out of sight.

The two well-dressed pawns in Eddie's game shut the doors on their oversized M5 and drove up the fancy pavers and back through the entrance, leaving the grounds and a marked man behind them. The gate closed, and Steve returned his focus back to the house, where everything was quiet for the time being.

He put down the scope and relaxed, taking advantage of the lull while the hot sun climbed closer to its high point. Steve figured he had approximately one hour to get to the location where Grace was picking him up.

Steve took a drink of water and rolled over onto his stomach to take one more peek. He noticed a dark gray unmarked Crown Vic creeping toward the front gate, the window open just enough to see the driver through the sun's glare. Steve's smile hit both ears when he saw who that someone was. He put the spotting scope into the backpack, zipped it up, and disappeared down the escape route he had mapped in his head.

Steve walked out from thick brush to see Grace pulled over on the side of the road, waiting with her blinker on. He got into the jet black Bentley GT, shut the door, and began discussing his eventful morning as they pulled away.

Chapter 22

Sean and I pulled up to the Jamestown address that Ned from Blue Skies had given to us, and gazed across the long field that surrounded the contemporary glass house like a smooth, quiet pond at dusk. I rolled down my window at the gate and pushed the black button on the intercom.

A voice shot out of the speaker. "Can I help you?"

"Providence Police," I said. "We would like to speak with Eddie Gomez, please."

I looked at Sean, who also had doubtful expectations of our entrance. To our mutual surprise, while I was thinking about putting it into reverse and leaving, the gate rolled open and allowed us onto the manicured grounds. As we approached the house, Eddie G. opened the front door and came strolling down the front walkway to greet us. He stopped at the conjunction of the driveway pavers and some jumbo cobblestones that made up a circle big enough to display a Mini Cooper.

We stepped across the cobbles and shook hands with the alleged Rhode Island drug kingpin.

"What can I do for you, Officers?" Eddie talked to us with no worry in his voice, as if we were there for donations.

"We would like to ask you about one of your rental properties."

"Okay, which one?"

"Baxton Street, over near the armory."

"The armory? Oh yeah, I know the one." He talked to us as if we were dumb and he was running the show. "So what do you want to know?"

"Gee, where should I start, Eddie? Maybe the house blowing up?" I slapped a bit of sarcasm his way. I already couldn't stand this guy.

"Oh, that. I try to screen these animals before they move in. What else can I do? I'm not their father." Eddie spread the shit on our toast extra thick as he spoke to us through his condescending grin.

"What about Brian Perez and Alex Reese?" Sean said. "What about your other boys that got snuffed out over on Wood Street? We know they were all with you."

The two of us were trying to have as much patience as possible in dealing with the jerk. He was incredibly full of himself and really needed an old-fashioned beating.

"They all rented from me," Eddie said smugly. "Of course I knew them. Listen, guys, I hate to cut you short, but I have a feeling that you should be talking to my lawyer, not me. Oh, and another thing." He pointed his finger at us as if it had some imaginary power behind it and spoke to us with brass balls big enough to fit in a dump truck. "I tried to cooperate with you guys, let you on my property and everything, but next time I think you should go through the proper channels if you're going to leave your jurisdiction."

"Hey, no problem, big shot!" I said, my veins pumping from the aggravation and adrenaline caused by this scumbag's disrespect. "Just remember, you'd better watch your back."

"Are you threatening me?"

"Not at all. I don't have to do a damn thing for you to get yours, dick!" I fired off with all the aggression that had built up from seeing Megan lying in her hospital bed.

"Get off my fucking property before I have your forty-thousand-a-year job, you fucking assholes!" Eddie screamed. His face turned red and angry, and the veins in his neck popped out.

I lost it. "Fuck you, punk! I'll break your fucking neck, you cocksucker!"

Sean put his arm across my chest to hold me back.

"What did you call me?" Eddie said, going wild as if I had just pulled a cord that started another engine.

Sean shoved me back to the car, yelling at me. "Let's go, Elliot! That's enough."

Eddie was still flipping out from a nerve that I'd obviously pinched. I started the car and moved toward the gate, which fortunately was still open.

"What the fuck was that, Elliot?" Sean said, looking at me under tightly knitted eyebrows.

"I'm sorry, man. That motherfucker just rubbed me the wrong way."

"You know that if he calls the station, we're screwed, right?" Sean threw his arms up in frustration as he turned and looked out the back window.

I cut across the center of the island with a trail of smoke billowing out of my ears like bullhorns on a Peterbilt. I replayed what had happened, but changed the ending to me crushing Eddie's head on his cobblestone walkway and stomping his teeth out with the heel of my Italian shoe.

By the time Sean and I got back into Providence, I'd convinced him that we should go snooping around some of Eddie's properties. He'd been against it at first, but like I told him, if we were going to catch shit for what happened that day, we might as well go all the way and make the ass-reaming worth it.

We stopped over at Lou's Garage to grab the Mustang at impound, but ended up with a late-model triple-white Maxima because the old pony we had been using was gone. We got in and headed over to Sean's house, so we could grab a quick bite to eat and change our clothes.

~~~

We got into character as a couple of wannabe thugs looking to seek out some employment under any of Eddie's enterprises.

I looked in the mirror at myself and had to laugh. "I look like a complete dick right now." Funny what clothes and a flat-brim hat can do to your appearance.

"Come on, you look good. The gold warm-up pants, the violet wifebeater—it looks great." Sean stuffed down the last of his turkey sandwich as he walked into the bathroom.

I wrote down over a dozen addresses on a piece of scrap paper and mapped out the order of which Gomez properties we were going to hit first. I folded it up and stuffed it into my pocket, and looked out the window and across the backyard. I saw a couple of kids riding their bikes with baseball gloves hanging from the handlebars. They rode by and disappeared behind the neighbor's fence.

I thought about all the different spots where my friends and I used to ride to and hang out. I also, once again, thought about how fast time flies by, and how no matter how hard you try, you cannot get that time back.

All my friends would want to eat at my house all the time because my mother always made everything special for us, like chicken cutlets, Italian grinders, cookies, and spinach pies. You name it, she made it.

"You ready?" Sean said, breaking up my memories of a great and innocent childhood.

"I've been ready, you slow bastard. What were you doing, jerking off in there?"

"We're going to be out all night. Can't I take my time to take a shit in my own house?" Sean yanked on his crotch, pulling on the ridiculous brown-and-orange gym pants.

"You look sharp, pal. I think you might get lucky tonight." I busted Sean's balls and pushed against his shoulder, bringing a smile to his Irish mug.

The two of us took off in our sporty new ride with our seats pushed as far back as they could go. We cruised our favorite grid that lay between Elmwood and Broad, with music that we'd never heard of playing and pulsating through the troubled streets.

We slowed down and crept by the first dump on the list. It seemed as if we'd broken up a little party by bringing our noses a bit too close, because three good-sized dudes brought themselves across the sidewalk and over to both front windows of the car.

A Spanish dude with two sleeves of jailhouse tats leaned in the passenger window and scoped out the car we knew he wanted to take from us. "You boys lost?"

"No, not at all. Actually, we were told Eddie G. was looking for some new talent on the street."

One of the baboons started to laugh, and the other two joined in like sheep.

"You two clowns have talent, wearing last year's colors. Please, Eddie G. wouldn't waste his time on two crackers like you. Now get out of the car, because we're taking this motherfucker." Mr. Tattoo flipped around a butterfly knife with some skill as he told us how he thought the night was going down.

I opened up the car door, and Eddie Gomez's six-foot, 200-pound Spanish officer grabbed me, but only for a split second. I kicked down on the side of his knee and then met his face with an uppercut that knocked him to the pavement. I hopped on him and threw this tough guy a monster beating, trying to teach him a lesson and put on a good show.

His two shadows finally decided to step in and help the lump of shit. Both of them pointed blades at me, threatening to end my life. I looked over to Sean, who was on the phone and signaling me to hurry up. I knew the call he was on must have been important.

I stood up, grabbed my snub-nosed from the pancake holster I was wearing under my ridiculous costume, and pointed it at the fools. "I'll drop you where you stand." I squeezed the trigger halfway to expose the hammer on the spurless .357 Magnum, showing them that I was very serious and would gun them down if I had to.

"Hey, come on, man. Not today." Sean opened his door and stood up as he slapped the roof, trying to talk me off a ledge the two guys thought was real.

I slowly brought the gun down beside my hip and released the tension on the trigger. "Yeah, maybe you're right. Today does seem like a fucked-up day."

The two assholes stood in front of me, still holding their hands high in the sky.

Sean got back in the car. "Come on. Let's go."

I climbed in the ride and left the trio in the road a bit dazed and confused by what had just happened to them.

I drove us to the next dump on the list while Sean filled me in on the phone call he'd received while I was having fun with Eddie's goobers.

"That was Jimmy on the phone," he said. "He wanted to tell us that he's talked to a few other departments. He spoke to some brother detectives that were able to fill him in with murders similar to ours, but they're all too far in the past. At this point, they're just stories. He's waiting on these guys to dig the files out of the archives and fax them over to us anyway."

"Did Jimmy mention any murder weapons?"

"No, he didn't get that far. He said he wanted to wait for the files."

"Did he mention hearing anything about Eddie calling in a complaint on us?"

"Nope. Who knows, maybe he's not going to call at all. Maybe we got lucky because he doesn't need any attention brought his way." Sean pointed to our next stop, where a young woman hung out in the breeze, waiting for a quick trick. "Look at this."

She turned and walked toward us, and in doing so took away our view of her barely covered ass cheeks. She strutted over with her hands on her hips. She bent over at Sean's window, snapping her gum, and gave the two of us a free shot of her girls, which hung in midair atop a pink lace bra. "Are you studs looking to party?"

I noticed her eyes look past us, exposing her pimp who was watching from the window of another of Eddie's houses across the street.

"What kind of party are you talking about?" Sean pulled cash out of his pocket, trying to keep her attention on our business.

"A party where the two of you can do anything you want to me." She dragged her long fake nails along her bottom lip, exposing her teeth, while ogling us with X-rated eyes.

"What's the rate?"

"A hundred apiece, and we can go upstairs and get started on the best half hour of your lives." The young hooker hiked her skirt up over her hips, exposing her matching panties.

"What if we're friends with Eddie G.?" Sean asked and winked. "Do we get a discount?"

She pulled her skirt back down over her hips, trying not to look at her boss who was watching the whole show. "I don't know what you're talking about, but I think you should get out of here." She backed off, giving us the middle finger. "Fuck you!"

Sean flipped her off right back as I pulled off the curb, leaving the whore behind.

As we drove, the streets became more and more crowded with illegal activities that spiked up the voltage meter. In the city, when the sun goes down, the darkness creeps in.

I passed by every house on the list to find that each one of them was a separate entity untraceable in the filling of Eddie's pockets. He probably collected the rent checks from Section 8 through the state, and if there was a bust on prostitution or drugs, he wouldn't even be in the equation.

As smart as our boy Eddie seemed, I had a feeling that if the vigilante was in fact after him, no one would be able to protect him from that madman's grip.

Chapter 23

Eddie and three of his men headed back from a business deal with a big fish who supplied most of the coke throughout the South Boston area and pieces of western Mass. The four men hammered down Route 95 South, passing around a bottle of Jack Daniels they had picked up for the ride back into Rhode Island.

Eddie set the cruise control and steered with one finger. He had a trunkful of coke and a gray leather gut full of drunken derelicts who together had enough alcohol content to blow a hot-air balloon from there to California.

Their car, filled with booze and banter, was almost taken out by a car that came out of nowhere and whipped in front of them. Eddie became hot with rage. His foot immediately buried the gas pedal, and his eyes fixed upon the midsized vehicle running ahead of him.

The car was quickly losing ground as the burgundy S-600 smoothly shifted into overdrive at a buck thirty while Eddie simultaneously shifted from disorderly and drunk to belligerent with a dangerous buzz. He cut from the low-speed lane across to the high-speed lane in the snap of a finger, as if he was changing lanes to grab a burger at McDonald's.

"Look at them swerve, Eddie. They must be shit-faced." Eddie's copilot pointed out the obvious.

Eddie approached the car like a lion chasing down a gazelle in the wild. He cut back across two lanes and headed right for the late-model Camry. He turned on his high beams and came straight down the driver's door, holding only inches between the two makes.

Eddie bullied the Camry into the breakdown lane and over the paved berm, putting it into a rain gutter, which pulled the ground right out from underneath the Toyota. The awkward predicament shot the car airborne across the cement chute. The silver four-door hit the other side of the half-pipe, catching the concrete top off-kilter, as the front tire of the Camry caught the wheel and caved in the front axle. The weight of the car countered, sending all four wheels flipping.

The vehicle shot roughly fifty feet across a weed-infested dirt gully and straight into the blade of a bulldozer that was parked off the side of the highway because of some road construction on the long stretch of interstate.

Eddie pulled up and stopped. The crew turned and gawked out the windows at two young boys who were definitely dead.

"I guess they won't be cuttin' anyone else off." Eddie laughed out loud and punched it, driving away while his guys stared out the back window at the desolate highway.

Eddie set the cruise control back to seventy-five and glared into the empty rearview mirror, smiling with satisfaction. He ordered his wingman to turn up the stereo, and with zero remorse, signaled the bartender for another drink. He turned the volume up high as "Rebel Yell" blared out of the speakers as if they were at a rock concert. The cap came off the bottle of whiskey, and the drinking picked up where they had left off, beginning with Eddie and making its way counterclockwise around the foursome.

~~~

As they floated through Providence with clear heads, Steve Krasson, wearing solid black from head to toe, hopped the fence at 171 Wetherill Road and slunk across the lawn. He moved toward Eddie's pad, which was well lit and heavily guarded with surveillance cameras, motion lights, and the two guard dogs that Steve had already seen in action. He silently approached the back door, where he pulled out his pack and took out a goody bag for Eddie's mutts. Then he quietly squeezed a small IV tube between the threshold and weather stripping of the door.

He turned on the valve that was connected to a bag full of hearty homemade chicken gravy that Grace had cooked the night before. He could see the two guard dogs sleeping as the tip of the plastic tube started to leak out onto the terrazzo floor.

Steve knocked on the door with his knuckle, waking up the hounds. They jumped up, barking, and were at the back door in a split second, ready to chew someone's ass. They started to sniff away at the scent of chicken as the thin, rich broth spread across the first tiles and into the grout lines of the shiny white-and-gray floor.

Steve knew he didn't have long, so he moved quickly along the backside of the house to scope out the rooms and see who was home. The guy and girl from the threesome were in the back corner room, sleeping with the television turned up loud enough for Steve to hear outside.

He moved to the front of the house, blending in with the darkness of the night, and hid behind a van in the driveway that belonged to Eddie's guys, who were on their way back and presently crossing the Jamestown Bridge. He reached in his pack and pulled out a block of C-4 that was pigtailed and ready to go. Steve rolled underneath the back of the van and wedged the package between the gas tank straps and a shock mount on the passenger side.

He rolled back out and followed the same path he'd taken on the way in, passing Eddie's lovers and then his dogs, who were still fully occupied with their late-night snack. He pulled the bag and tube from them as he passed by and picked up speed. He jolted to the fence, jumped up and over, and ran back to the spotting scope equipped with night vision that he had set up in the darkness.

Steve snagged the giant peeper and looked through the scope while patiently waiting to see what happened. He grabbed a cell phone out of the side pocket of his backpack and looked up into the sky. He thought about how many times he had been in that same situation, and about all the people he had whacked in his career. He felt proud of his life's work, knowing he had saved hundreds, maybe thousands, of people from some type of pain brought on by criminals like Eddie.

Steve thought about his parents, who had been T-boned as they passed through a green light while holiday shopping in the city. The two thugs involved in the hit-and-run were high as kites off speedballs and managed to walk away from the wreck, while Steve's mother and father bled out in their green family sedan.

His eyes filled with pain from memories of his parents that barely existed anymore. He closed his eyes, draining his tears, which were then swallowed up by his thick scruff.

His blurry vision returned to see Eddie's guys stumbling over to the van. Steve dialed in the scope and watched Eddie's loud and obnoxious pissants urinate all over the side of the van.

Steve turned his focus to Eddie, who stepped out of his car and began to stagger toward his house. He watched Eddie laugh and point at his three buddies as they climbed into the dark blue Chevy van. The headlights of the van illuminated a small circumference around the vehicle, and the brake lights bounced off Eddie, giving Steve an even clearer picture.

The van sat at the gate for almost a minute before the guys realized that the gate was still open. Eddie threw his arms up and laughed at the drunken stupidity of the three idiots, who probably couldn't tie their shoes at the moment. The driver hit the gas a little heavy and peeled out in the loose stone where the driveway met the road.

Steve hit SEND on the cheap throwaway phone he'd picked up at a gas station in the middle of nowhere a year ago. With a breath of intent in the air, the van exploded. The blast forced the van up off the ground, and it landed on its side, engulfed in flames.

With a big smile, Steve watched Eddie fall to his knees as his roommates ran around the house in complete chaos, along with the dogs, who were barking and going wild. Eddie struggled to his feet and ran out to the trunk of his fancy sedan, grabbed two duffel bags, and brought them inside.

Steve packed up his gear and moved through the thick patch of grass with the help of the moonlight shining down on the land and water that lay calm and peaceful. He maneuvered through the almost impossible terrain as if it was second nature, leaving disruption and disrespect behind at the big kingpin's new summer getaway.

Chapter 24

Sirens from Fire and Rescue wailed across the land as Steve made his escape. The trucks pulled up to the gate, where the van still burned, a few minutes behind the town police. Steve looked at his watch, impressed with the quick timing of local municipalities.

He spotted the dark car sitting on the shoulder, running and ready to go, so he hopped out of the thick and scampered across the road while turning a couple 360s out of caution. He jumped in and shut the door, and Grace shifted into drive and pulled away from the mayhem, leaving Eddie in a world of shit that would keep him up at night, wondering if he'd be next.

"That was beautiful," a voice said from the backseat. The cherry from a cigar pierced the darkness as it burned hot with a long drag of enthusiasm.

"I try my best." Steve sat forward and clipped the seatbelt buckle behind him, succumbing to the annoying chime telling him to do so. "I survived four fucking years in Vietnam, hanging from Hueys in midair, getting shot at from hot LZs. I have seventy-seven confirmed kills from ranges of over five hundred meters and dozens of stealth kills with my blade while living in the stinky, wet, gook-infested jungle, and I have to wear a fucking seatbelt!"

A hand reached out and tapped Steve on the shoulder with a cigar, interrupting his little meltdown over the seatbelt law. He grabbed the rich maduro and dragged it under his nose, taking it in. He closed his eyes and let his senses take the wheel down a much cooler path. Steve lit the torpedo, illuminating the front seat, then cracked his window and watched the big cloud disappear as it got sucked out of the car and dissipated into the pores of the atmosphere.

Grace flipped on the high beams as they rambled through the blackness on back roads, making their way across the island and back to the bridge. They crossed over the peak, high above the bay, and began pointing downward, back toward North Kingstown. Steve stared at Quonset Point as it glowed in the distance all by itself. He followed the shoreline as it merged with the murk the city of Providence sat upon at the end of the skyline. He took a drag off the cigar and held it up to look at the gray ash. It was bending, but strong. He blew out a mouthful of smoke that bit at his senses but had cut his tension down a few notches.

"It's a hell of a smoke, isn't it?" the voice projected from the backseat.

"It's unbelievable, my friend." Steve laughed, thinking back to the van and wondering what Eddie was doing.

~~~

Eddie was dealing with the local police and a state trooper who had been nearby when the call came in.

He told the trooper and the Jamestown police sergeant in charge a load of bullshit to get them out of there as quickly as possible. "They were maintenance men that I used for my properties in the city. They were working late because they got here late."

What was left of the van got pulled up onto a flatbed at the end of Eddie's driveway, putting the explosive debacle to bed. All of the authorities packed up and moved on, and the lights disappeared up the road, with Jamestown Police at the end of the caravan.

Eddie stood in his driveway, looking at the fresh wound to his property. It could be fixed by the landscapers, but would scar his ego.

He walked to his house and shut the front door behind him, locked the deadbolt and set the alarm system, and glared out the window, reeling with paranoia. He stopped at the doorway to the room where his roommates, Jay and Courtney, were cuddled up with fear. They looked up to him, searching for some type of fatherly guidance. He turned and walked away from them with no emotions or words to convey, and sealed off the day by closing the door to his bedroom.

He lay down, gun on his chest, and grabbed his phone off the glass nightstand beside him. Eddie viewed half a dozen missed calls from one of his street employees, Mario S., and placed a call back to him. All of the day's events began to catch up with him, and curiosity swirled around in his head like a whirlwind.

Mario answered on the first ring. "What's up?"

"Six calls in ten minutes, Mario?" Eddie asked, ready for the worst. "What's wrong?"

"A couple of guys were all up on a bunch of your properties tonight, asking a lot of questions about working for you."

"So what? We might need some new bodies after tonight."

"Even if they're five-o?"

Mario's words punched Eddie square in the chest and lit up his quiet, heavy eyes. "What makes you think they were cops?"

"Toni saw one of these motherfuckers driving away in an unmarked the other day, when Luther Brice got shot trying to throw that baby from the window and shit."

"Ask Toni the color and make of the car." As Eddie waited, he got up from his bed and hopped onto the computer.

He typed *Luther Brice Providence Police* into his search bar, and the tragic but heartfelt story popped up on-screen. Eddie scanned through an article and discovered that a young detective, an ex-marine, had killed Luther with a single shot to the head, using a sniper rifle.

"Eddie, Toni says he thinks it was a gray Crown Vic."

Mario's news made Eddie's eye twitch, and the wheels in his polluted brain slipped into production. This had all started right in his own driveway.

Eddie did a little detective work of his own. "What did these guys look like?"

"The driver, around six foot, two hundred pounds, and the other guy, a few inches shorter, and maybe a buck eighty-five. The driver kicked the shit out of Willie. He's an Italian guy, and his partner is Irish or English or something like that."

That gave Eddie enough of a foundation to start constructing a box for whoever was responsible.

"Okay, thanks. Later, Mario," Eddie said and hung up the phone.

He found a *Providence Journal* write-up about the bank robbery and read the story about the two guys who were found dead in their getaway car. His emotions boiled over with anger when he read the names of the two men, especially the backseat shooter, who happened to be his cousin Jose.

"This is a big cover-up from Providence Police, and that guinea detective is behind it all!" Eddie screamed to the four walls. His two dogs lowered their heads and tucked their tails.

He continued down the paragraph, sorting through the mumble and textbook writing, until he came to the three victims shot during the robbery. The two dead bank employees were insignificant, but the survivor was a thirty-two-year-old woman who was engaged to a Providence police detective. Eddie's heart skipped a beat. He mulled the facts, taking mental notes and putting together a plan that would get him squared up with his new backbiter, Detective Frantallo.

Eddie shut off his laptop and got ready for bed. While brushing his teeth, he looked at his nickel revolver sitting next to the keyboard and wiped the tears off his face with his other hand.

He sank into bed, and all the emotions he'd been holding back began to strike at him, all the anger and denial from his own personal wounds.

Memories of Teddy, his friend and lover, who was his copilot back from
Southie tonight, lingered in the peaks and valleys of Eddie's mind as he
lay on his side and squeezed his pillow, revenge running through his
veins.

Chapter 25

I lay in bed, trying to contain the heaviness that pushed against the walls of my oath and my honor. The bright white beams of a pair of headlights flashed through my window and crossed over the wall at the foot of my bed, rousing my curiosity and suspicions. I eased out of bed and peeked out the window to see a car driving away and Jack walking up his porch steps before disappearing into his dim house.

Maybe he's been hanging out with Janice, I thought to myself. I walked backward and sat on the edge of the bed, wishing Megan were here to help me with this bout of insomnia. I looked at myself in the mirror, not knowing what to think or do.

My phone vibrated with a text from Megan's sister, Denise, letting me know that Megan was still in a coma, but that her vitals were climbing and she had started to move every so often. I got dressed after reading the good news. Besides, at that point, I knew I'd feel better if I just got up, instead of trying to go back to bed.

After a shower and a couple of soft-boiled eggs, I glanced over at the wall clock, which read 4:52 a.m. I rinsed my plate, finished my orange juice, and grabbed my dark roast, and then I walked out the door. The cool and still dark morning air held a certain mystique as the sun waited just around the corner.

Driving to the hospital felt almost surreal, with the soft colors and kind strokes of the quiet, early morning streets, the different angles and shapes, and the intermittent neon signs that stay lit all night, every night. The same streets would soon be flooded with chaos and clutter, and everything would take a beating from the swarms going about their same agendas all over again.

I passed by the empty guard shack and into the parking lot of the hospital, wondering when Megan was going to wake up and come home to me. I finished my last sip of coffee and threw the empty cup in the trash can outside the big glass entrance. The lobby was quiet, like the streets. I saw only two other people, both employees, as I walked through to the elevator.

I laughed to myself when I peeked in the room and saw Denise sleeping in the bed with Megan. The two sisters, like Frick and Frack, were inseparable, the best of friends. Thank God that Meg had Denise, because I would have been lost without her help through all this.

My phone started to blow up, so I glanced at the screen and took a few steps back into the corridor to answer. "What's up, Sean?"

"Elliot, sorry to call so early, but there was a big explosion at Eddie G.'s house."

Volts of energy passed right through the phone and stabbed me with intent. "Was he part of the explosion?"

"I know what you're thinking, but you're not that lucky. Although three of his contractors went up with the explosion and fried right in front of him."

"What time did this happen?"

"I talked with Billy Harriday, who was actually first on the scene. He told me he arrived around two thirty. He actually saw the explosion from a distance."

"So that means his response was pretty much immediate."

"I'd say so."

"I'm at the hospital, Sean. I'm gonna spend a few more minutes here and then go to the station to catch up on a few things. I'll see you there."

"Okay, man. Later."

I put away my phone and joined the Wilson sisters. I sat on the side of the bed for a time, holding Meg's hand, and then I kissed her good-bye. I hated to cut my visit short again, but Sean's phone call had drilled a pit in my stomach that I had to deal with. I planned to be back at the end of the day, so I decided not to wake Denise.

I got into my car, noticing the first run of morning traffic had started to pick up, and leaned forward to turn the key to start the engine. The reflection of a car in my side mirror caught my eye—a car that I remembered from the escapade the night before. The driver of the mid-2000s Jeep with after-market five-star wheels, which had been parked across the street from the hooker we'd visited, saw me notice him and held up a big middle finger.

I pulled out of the lot with my head in the clouds, about to play a game that the fuckhead behind me had no idea how to play. After a few minutes and a few strategic moves, I ended up in his rearview mirror, calling in the registration on the hunter green SUV. I watched his head wobble back and forth with uncertainty over what his next move would be.

The registration came back to CTI Maintenance, which I was sure was one of Eddie G.'s ghost companies. I flipped on the wigwags and hit the siren. After I had leaned on the air horn a couple of times, the driver put on his blinker and pulled off the wide, single-lane road. I opened the door and got out at the red light. The predator had become the prey.

I approached the ass end of the vehicle. The windows were tinted, but I was still able to see through to the front seat. No passenger.

"Let me see your hands outside the door!" I announced with a stern tone and grit in my voice. "Don't move, driver. Open the door from the outside of the car and slowly step out." I sidestepped as I approached the Jeep, and moved out into the street with my gun drawn and ready to fire. "Four fifty-one, I need backup at the intersection of South Main and Wickenden," I said into my radio. I waited for confirmation as I watched the driver's every move.

"Units will be assisting you right away," dispatch replied.

I put the radio back in my coat pocket and brought my left hand back up on the gun.

The middle-aged man got out of the car and dropped down to his knees with his hands on top of his head, obviously no stranger to this procedure. He was wearing a dirty wifebeater tank and had at least a dozen homemade tats covering both arms and shoulders. I looked over his hands and into the Jeep, where I could see an Uzi stuffed between the console and driver's seat.

Sergeant Tommy Graham, Major Sullivan's nephew, was first on scene. He flew out of his car to assist me and attempted to put cuffs on this maggot who I was sure was an illegal alien. Tommy got one cuff on the man's left hand, but lost control when the guy stepped back with everything he had and pinned Tommy against the front fender. He shifted his weight, bent his knees, and from the front balls of his feet fired straight up like a rocket and smashed Tommy directly under his chin. Tommy went down like a ton of bricks, and this smartass then charged me full force like a defensive lineman.

I held out my compact .45 and moved to the side to avoid the collision, trying to talk this idiot out of doing something really stupid. He lost his balance on a sewer cover that had settled crooked, and slipped. He told me he wouldn't go back and would rather die first, then pulled a small belly gun from his waistband and raised it straight at me. I snapped off three rounds into his chest as if he was a pin cushion and dropped him right in the middle of the road.

I scanned the area and saw that it had become crowded with pointing spectators, in shock from the display of violence that had just taken place during the early morning commute. This asshole lay in the middle of the road less than a hundred feet away from people who were having coffee and Danish, just a stone's throw away from my own house, with his chest like a piece of Swiss cheese.

I started to think about having two kills in one week. I highly doubted that I was going to be considered a hero on this one.

"I saw the whole thing," Sean said, tapping my shoulder.

"Sean! What are you doing here?"

"I was over on Hope and Waterman when the call came over the radio. I came as quick as I could."

"What the fuck was I supposed to do? The guy drew on me." I wiped the sweat off my face with my sleeve and looked up at the changing sky.

Intermittent sprinkles and a couple of thunder booms rattled the city. Miranda Kemp pulled up and got out of her cruiser, and the skies opened up with a flash storm that put a sudden stop to all conversation. I shut the door to my car, and the three of us ran for cover under an awning at the entrance of a pizza joint I ate in at least twice a week.

We watched the street move by us and bounce off car tires as well as the dead body that lay like a boulder in the middle of a thriving river.

"Is that the Jeep that was over on Sacket when we were talking with that hooker?" Sean asked.

"Definitely," I said. "He was waiting for me outside the hospital before all this happened."

The downpour slowed up, and the clouds started to separate and quickly broke apart, exposing the sun again. Miranda shook her head with compassion and wished me luck, gave me a tight hug, and then she got in her cruiser and took off to a three-car pileup that had just come in.

"This is the job, kid," Jack said as he walked up behind Sean and me. "I told you a million times that things are changing, and for the worst. You're probably gonna get shit for this one. Everything is trickling back to the station as we speak. They're saying you're a vigilante, not a cop. It's going to start spreading around that building like the bubonic plague, and in less than five minutes, your phone will be going off to get your ass downtown so someone can evaluate why you shot yet another killer."

"Maybe being a cop was a bad idea for me. Maybe I should've just stayed in the Corps." My phone rang. "Here we go, Jack. Less than two minutes." I answered the call that had come up as private. "Hello?" I hoped it was Major Sullivan and not one of the dicks from IID.

"You played it better than I could've dreamed of, you stupid prick cop!"

"Who the fuck is this?" I screamed into the phone at the caller who'd already hung up on me. "Hello? Hello!"

"Who was that, Elliot?" Jack asked.

"I think this asshole Eddie G. is after me. Sean and I have been snooping around his shit, plus I got into an argument with him at his house and told him I'd kill him."

"Who, that punk Gomez?"

I nodded, and my phone started to ring again, this time from a station line that was showing up on the caller ID. "Hello?"

"Elliot, what the fuck is going on?" Sullivan shouted from the other end.

"I don't know, Major. The guy I shot was waiting for me outside the hospital. He pulled a pistol on me and was about to shoot me. What the hell was I supposed to do?"

"It's not that, Elliot. It's the fact of two in one week. Most guys have a full career without having to fire their service weapon on duty. You have two kills in less than a week, and God knows what else lingering out in the woodwork that the department doesn't know about."

"I think this thug drug dealer I've somehow pissed off is behind this entire shit show and is now after me."

"Who? Eddie Gomez? Oh my God. Of all the cuckoo clocks, you pick that motherfucker to tangle assholes with? This prick has the best lawyers money can buy, Elliot!"

Jack bumped my arm, interrupting the phone call. I covered the receiver with my hand so Sullivan couldn't hear.

"I was thinking about what you said about the guy over there," Jack said. "That he was waiting for you at the hospital."

"Yeah, what about him?"

"Are you sure he was there for you, and not Megan?"

I started to think about Jack's speculation while the major ranted in my ear, waiting for a response. "Major, I'm really sorry, but I gotta go." I hung up on Major Sullivan with an unsettling sickness making its way through my entire body.

Jack jumped in with me, leaving Sean and a few other uniformed guys to clean up the mess I'd made. We screamed up Sheldon Street and whipped onto Brook Street sideways, almost slamming into the traffic jam that sat in front of us at the Wickenden Street intersection. I threw the lights on and bullied my way through the midmorning commute, having to rub a few garbage cans along with a street sign that I left a little cocked and crooked.

A clearing opened up on the wrong side of the street, so I moved over and punched it. I almost lost control sideways as I picked up speed on the roads that were still wet and slick from the storm. I blasted through a puddle right before the Point Street Bridge and hydroplaned, which sprayed dingy street water onto my windshield, blinding me, and forced me to flip on the wipers.

Jack sat quietly, pulling off the cigar, and took in the day's events, adding them to his long list of crazy life experiences. We flew over the bridge and were almost airborne from the swale in the road as we approached the busy intersection ahead. I put the brakes to the mat and came skidding in sideways to a dead stop.

"Fucking shit, get the fuck off the road!" I screamed out the window. I couldn't shake the sick feeling in my gut that Megan was in trouble.

I squeezed through the middle of the overstuffed intersection, surprisingly with no casualties, and headed south to the hospital as fast as I could go.

"Come on, come on, pick up." The phone rang in my ear, then clicked over to Denise's voice mail. "Denise, call me if you get this. It's an emergency." I hung up the phone as I pulled into the raised lot at full speed, turning a few heads as I bottomed out the front bumper and undercarriage. "Fuck! Jack, you stay down here just in case you see anything fucked up."

I pulled up to the emergency entrance and flung the door open with the assistance of my foot. I ran at a full sprint, weaving and dodging the now-busy lobby full of people. I hit the stairwell, not wanting to wait at the overcrowded elevator. I ran up three flights and opened the door as I downshifted a couple gears.

I entered the hallway as casually as possible, not wanting to draw any attention to myself. I passed the elevator, and it opened up with a ding, making me turn around. Denise walked out with a coffee, some cranberry juice, and a magazine folded under her right arm.

"Elliot, what's wrong?" she said.

"You have no idea. Have you seen anyone suspicious walking around here?"

"No, I've been in the room since you left. I know you think I was asleep when you were here earlier, but I woke up when you came in."

"How long has she been alone?"

"Just five minutes. I went to the cafeteria to grab a coffee when Krista came in to check on her ... What's wrong, Elliot? You're freaking me out." She looked over my shoulder and pointed up the hallway to Megan's room. "Why is that nurse wearing basketball sneakers and a five-o'clock shadow?"

The poser nurse took off when Denise spotted him.

"Hey you, stop right there!" I ran to Megan's room as he sailed around the corner, slid, and grabbed the doorjamb to keep from falling.

I noticed that Megan's IV bag was cloudy. It didn't look right. And whatever this guy had put in there was making its way down the tube that fed into her arm.

"Elliot, who was that nurse?" Denise screamed as she ran into the room behind me, completely panicked and hysterical, dropping the drinks all over the floor.

I tore the IV out of Meg's arm and threw it on the floor. "That IV is poison. Tell the nurses to save it for evidence and have them get her a new one." I flew out of the room, hoping I could catch the piece of shit who had just tried to kill my fiancée.

I hit the stairwell and tore down the floors, skipping three steps at a time. I heard the door to the lobby swing shut, so I jumped off the last bunch of stairs, slammed into the door, and then jerked it open to see the gift shop across from me. On my right was a normal, undisturbed hallway. I then focused my attention to my left, where I saw a young girl helping an elderly woman up off the floor.

I ran over to them. "Did a manly looking nurse knock you over?"

"Yeah, he went that way," the girl said, pointing down the hallway.

I picked up my pace to a full sprint as I headed to the east wing, scanning across the glass windows as I ran, looking for any type of ruckus. I pressed out the nearest exit and looked around for anything that might catch my eye. Everything looked normal, so I turned around and left it behind.

I rode the elevator back up so I could catch my breath, and walked into Megan's room, now crowded with nurses. They were all startled by what had happened, but had control of the situation.

"Keep that bag right here," I ordered the nurses, showing my credentials. I dialed up Jimmy to get him there pronto. "Jimmy, I need you to come to the hospital immediately." I explained the situation to him, dropping at least a dozen F-bombs. "Can you also get a badge to sit outside Megan's room?" I hung up with Jimmy and hugged Denise, who was a complete mess.

"I can't leave the room, Elliot. I won't!" She broke down and tears poured from her eyes as she held me tight, feeling responsible because she had left her sister alone for a few minutes.

I grabbed her shoulders firmly. "Listen to me. This is not your fault. Keep an eye on her, and call me if anyone or anything doesn't look right. My buddy Jimmy's coming here, and he's gonna have an officer sit outside this room. I have to go, Denise. Remember, anything that doesn't look right, you tell the badge. He'll be sitting right outside the door."

My nerves were clawing at my every extremity, making it hard to keep my composure as I walked back down to Jack and to what lay ahead of me for the rest of the day.

I walked out of the emergency exit, where two paramedics almost ran me over as they wheeled in a man on a stretcher, screaming for a doctor's help. One of the paramedics was holding a ball of gauze, already saturated in blood, to the side of the man's head. As they rolled the victim away down the hall, I caught a look at his sneakers. They started to shake as the man went into convulsions. I ran after them as they headed around the corner toward the ER.

When I finally caught up to them at the doors to the ER, I pulled the thin sheet off the victim and saw that the man was wearing a nurse's outfit. I nudged the paramedic to the side and looked into the man's eyes, which were bugging out of his head. A doctor stuck a long needle into his chest and yelled at me to back off.

I looked at the loop ring in the guy's right ear, opposite his wound. I pushed the paramedic aside who was getting in my face and lifted up the victim's sleeve, exposing the tattoos that belonged to the asshole from the night before.

"You got what you deserve, you fucking maggot!" I whispered in his ear, projecting all my anger and hatred into his eyes.

"Call the police, right now!" the doctor yelled out.

I turned and ran down the hall. I blasted through the emergency exit, but saw a Taurus station wagon parked in the spot where I had left the car and Jack. I heard a horn blow from the backside of the lot and followed the sound to see my car and Jack's arm out the window, waving to me. I ran through the parking lot and got into my car, which was already running and ready to go.

Two cruisers sped up the road and squealed into the entrance that I had just used for my exit. I pulled away from the hospital and got on Route 95 South. I crossed over into the high-speed lane as I held my forehead and pulled on my hair, trying to figure out what the hell had happened in the past two hours.

"Some guy I ran into the other night just tried to poison Megan, right in her room." I said to Jack, breaking my rage-filled silence.

"I knew something was wrong."

"Then, as I was walking out, the same guy got rolled in with a trauma wound to the side of the head."

Jack sent off a text. "Is Megan all right?"

"She's all right, Jack, but might not be if you hadn't been with me today. Just one minute later, and she would've been dead."

Jack lit his cigar. "Well, I'm just glad she's okay."

I looked at Jack through the corner of my eye as he stared out the side window. I felt funny asking him why he'd moved the car at the hospital, but I couldn't help wondering if it had really been coincidence that the guy I'd been chasing had come back in on his deathbed. I guessed, in the big picture, what difference did it make if Jack had done it? The prick got what he had deserved.

I pulled my phone out of my pocket and looked at the call coming in as I tried to keep my eyes on the road. "Jimmy, what's up, man?"

"Elliot, that was pure sodium hydroxide that was injected into Megan's IV. If you hadn't come in and ripped it out when you did, she'd be gone."

"Is it traceable?"

"It's way too common to trace."

I clenched my teeth in frustration. "The guy who's responsible is in the ER right now."

"Yeah, one of the doctors called us to complain that someone, maybe a cop, was harassing a patient. When we got here, Megan's sister filled us in, so we put two and two together."

"Good, at least you got him."

"No, we don't. The genius who attempted the hit on Megan died just a few minutes ago."

"Now, that's a shame." I said, smirking.

"The boys are down here circling around this place like vultures, Elliot. Your rough start to the day has turned the whole department upside down. You know I'm on your side, man. I don't give a shit how many of these dirtbags you kill. But unfortunately, I'm not in charge of that."

"What happened to the guy that tried to kill Megan?"

"His head was smashed against a bollard in the side alley of the hospital."

"Wow, that's pretty harsh." I glanced over at Jack, still looking out the window and puffing on his morning smoke.

"By the way, I've received information on over a dozen cases of the same type of murders with the same type of wound entry as our infamous eardrum popper. The weird thing is, the last one, according to all records, was in 1988."

"That is weird. Have you talked to Sean?"

"Oh yeah, he told me all about it. IID is going to say you're a trigger-happy cop. You know they don't give a shit about you or Megan."

"Nevertheless, Eddie G. is who sent that guy, and now I have to do what I have to do, department or no department."

"Are you sure Eddie G. is behind all of this?" Jimmy said after a brief pause.

"Definitely."

"I don't know, this is turning into a real nightmare. Major Sullivan is getting his ass reamed right now."

"I know, man, but when people fuck with my family, or me, I have to protect what's mine. I don't know . . . I just can't help it. Maybe I should turn in my badge."

"C'mon, Elliot, don't give me that guilt trip garbage. You're a great cop, and I know what you're saying. Hell, I'm not disagreeing with you. Look, I can't tell you how to feel or to roll over and let people walk all over you. I can tell you one thing, though. The department doesn't want this kind of publicity saddling up on their backs. I just don't want to see you get screwed because you decided to go up against a lunatic like Eddie G."

"I appreciate that, Jimmy. You and Sean always have my back, and you know I have yours. I'll call Major Sullivan right now and try to explain myself."

"Call me if you need anything, bud."

"I will, Jimmy. Thanks, man." I hung up with Jimmy and immediately called Major Sullivan.

Sullivan scorned me with daggers right off the bat. "You'd better not hang up on me again, Detective!"

"I apologize, sir, but if I hadn't, Megan would be dead right now. So, I hate to say this, but I would do it again if it meant saving her life."

"Listen, Elliot, I'm on your side. I'm not telling you not to do your job, but to tone it down a little. I'll clean up this mess for the time being, because once again there are all types of witnesses and even surveillance cameras that confirm the guy you pulled over drew a piece on you this morning. I don't give a fuck what IID says, it was you or him, one hundred percent self-defense. But what the hell is this other thing at the hospital, and when is this all going to stop?"

"The guy who got his head smashed in put lye into Megan's IV bag."

"Did you smash his head?"

"I swear to you, Major, I wanted to, and maybe even would've if I'd caught him, but I did not kill that guy."

"Okay, listen, you come into the station and come see me, right away."

"I'll be there in twenty minutes." I hung up the call as I pulled up in front of Jack's house.

Jack opened the door, stepped out, and leaned his head in through the car window. "Don't worry, Elliot. Everything's gonna work out." He shut the door, turned his back, and walked up his porch stairs.

Chapter 26

Someone was knocking at my front door. I opened my eyes and looked over at my alarm clock to see it flashing twelve even. I picked up my phone, but it was dead. I had forgotten to charge it after coming home last night.

The knocking grew louder.

"Shit, I'm coming, I'm coming!" I yelled as I ran to the door. I opened it to find Jack's fist in midair, ready to start banging away again.

"Elliot, what the fuck are you doing?" Jack followed me in and shut the front door behind him. "Sean's been trying to call you all morning. They need you to come in and clear some stuff for IID."

"What time is it?" I threw yesterday's rags back on because I had no clean work clothes.

"It's quarter to ten. Someone got all liquored up last night and hit a pole at the corner of South Main Street. It knocked out a transformer."

"I was having a crazy dream, Jack. Plus, I got home late last night because I stopped by the hospital to make sure everything was okay." I put some wax in my hair and pulled it back, trying to cut as many corners as possible to get to the station quickly. "Fucking hell, this shit has me all fucked up, and Megan not pulling out of this coma is wearing on me."

I headed out, skipping breakfast and a shave, and without picking up the mess yet again that had started to build up in my neglected house.

"Why don't you come over tonight and have a nice cigar and some vino?" Jack said as I backed into the street and threw it in drive.

"All right, sounds good. I'll see you later." I nailed it up the thin historical street.

I people-watched out the driver's side window for fun until I saw a young girl, roughly fifteen or sixteen years old, sitting on the corner of Benefit and John streets, holding her shirt up with a look of straight suicide plastered all over her face. I pulled up to the curb, right before the stop sign, and put my car in park. I got out and was about to walk across the street when a silver Astro van whipped up on the wrong side of the road and the side door slid open.

The curtain in the front window of the corner house moved, which led me to believe I'd been made. The young girl looked at me with confusion on her face and started to scream for help.

I pulled out my sidearm as a guy stepped out of the van. "Don't move a fucking muscle." I walked toward the situation, keeping focus on the three dirtbags still inside the van. "Get out of the fucking van, right now!" I yelled with a coarseness and rigidity that stopped everyone for two blocks.

The prick on the sidewalk dived back into the van, yelling to get out of there, and the driver punched the van in reverse down the steep hill. The passenger pulled out a Mac-10 and hung out the window, pointing it at the young girl.

"Look out!" I yelled to her as the thug opened fire, laying bullets up the incline of the sidewalk and into the side of the house, the fence, and ultimately her left leg.

I rested my elbow against the light post on the corner and dumped my clip into the front of the van. With my clip almost empty, I hit the shooter, making him drop his handheld automatic assault weapon onto the road. The van managed a half-ass Rockford at the bottom of the hill and sped away, with holes from a clip full of bullets in the front end and one of their own injured.

I yelled out for someone to call 911 as I ran over to the hysterical young girl. I pulled off my necktie and wrapped up her leg to slow the bleeding while I tried to comfort her and bring her heart back down to a normal thump. "What's your name?"

"Stephanie." She clenched her teeth from the obvious pain as tears ran down her face.

"Stephanie, what were you doing over here, and who are those guys?"

"Those guys own me."

"What do you mean they 'own' you?"

"I have no family. They take care of me as long as I do what they say."

"How old are you?" I checked the bleeding, which had slowed up a bit.

"I'm sixteen. My mom died of a drug overdose last year, and I have nobody."

"Why are you on this particular corner?" I asked and heard a car start up in the driveway of the house we were sitting next to.

"Because I have sex with this man every Wednesday." She pointed to the brick-faced extravagant home with a fancy stone foundation and front steps.

"It's Thursday."

"Yeah, I know. I stay the night."

"Stay right here." I got up and walked over to the car as it backed out of the driveway and into the street.

"Roll the window down," I announced to the man driving the car.

He rolled his window down with attitude. "What do you want?" His shitty tone sent out a tough-guy signal that just fueled the engine inside me.

"Pull back in your driveway, and get out of the car."

"Fuck you, asshole." He put it in drive, but a cruiser and ambulance showed up simultaneously and blocked him in.

His face turned beet red. "Tell them to move, right now."

"Sir, get out of the car," I said again.

"Do you know who I am?"

"No, sir, I don't."

"I'm House Representative George Staten, you fucking idiot!"

"Yeah, and I'm Detective Elliot Frantallo. Get out of the fucking car, right now!" I screamed as my patience thinned out, which caused Rescue and the patrolman to pull focus onto my newest problem.

The man put the car into park and got out in the middle of the road. Traffic had started to back up around this midmorning debacle just five blocks away from my home.

"I guess you don't like your job too much." George Staten threw around his weight with what to me were empty threats.

"Oh, I think you're the only one here that's in trouble, my friend." I grabbed his arm and began to read him his rights.

"Don't touch me, asshole." He ripped his arm away from me and took a quick swing.

My head, chock-full of bullshit from the previous three days, fired off the wrong signal, and I acted on pure aggression.

I dodged his weak attempt by ducking down, and rose up with anger, adrenaline, and an uppercut that knocked Representative Staten on his ass, seeing stars. I picked his sorry ass up off the ground and cuffed him while reading him his rights.

At that point, his wife came running out into the road, yelping and calling me every name under the sun as she threatened to sue me, shoot me, kill me, and own me. The ambulance pulled away with Stephanie packed up in the back, while the street filled up with more cruisers.

I threw George in the back of a marked car as Major Sullivan pulled up. He got out of his ride and took off his sunglasses, revealing eyes that told me more than I wanted to know.

He fingered me over. "Do you know who that is in the backseat?"

"Yeah, he already told me."

"So, then, what happened?" At least he was letting me convey my side first.

I gave Major Sullivan a play-by-play as the husband-and-wife team yelled and filled the streets with swagger.

"Mitch, I want this man fired immediately," Mrs. Staten, furious and ready to cut my jugular, ordered Major Sullivan.

"Sheila, please, go inside and let me do my job."

She got into George's Lexus, still parked in the middle of the street, and took off, almost hitting us in the process.

"Look at that crazy bitch! She needs to get arrested with him."

"Leave her alone, Elliot."

"She almost hit us."

"But she didn't. Trust me. It's easier to just ignore her." Sullivan rolled his eyes and walked back to his car, hands on his hips. "Get me this report right away!"

"What was I supposed to do?" I called after him. "Nothing? Just ignore this little girl and the pieces of shit who were whacking her every day? You know what? I'm done. I can't take this shit anymore." I walked away from the conversation and got into my car, ready to throw in the towel. I grabbed my phone and called Sean as I took off. "Come on, Sean, pick up."

"Elliot, where the hell have you been all morning?"

I held the phone pressed tight against my ear. "Sean, I think I might be in some deep shit."

"Yeah, I know, I just heard about Representative Staten. You not only arrested a state rep, but also busted his nose."

"He swung at me first."

"He's pressing charges on you!"

The light on College Hill turned green. I pulled up on my blinker, changing my mind, and drove straight through the intersection. "Sean, I gotta go." I pressed END on my phone and headed away from work and all the bullshit that I was sure was funneling me toward a suspension.

I carted down the street that I had first called home when I got back from ten years as a marine. My parents, who had since moved to Florida, had taken care of a little cottage-style house that sat between two monster homes at the end of Benefit Street. My mother's aunt had lived there a better part of her life, and when she passed away, my mom and my uncle Domenic rented it to college kids until I came along. When my parents decided to move down south, they sold the house, which forced me to move. That's when I started renting from and found a great friend in Jack.

I walked away from the house and toward my old cigar hangout, where I had received an education on many different little bits and pieces of this city and its people. Lenny rounded the corner with the hose dragging behind him as he watered all his hanging plants, getting them ready for the sunshine that would peek through the tall trees in about another hour.

He caught me out of the corner of his eye and greeted me with open arms when he realized it was me. "It's great to see you again! Twice in one week?"

"Do you have a few minutes to sit down and talk?" I asked, really needing some unbiased advice.

"Of course, my friend. Sit down. Sit down right over here." He patted a chair outside his shop and ducked inside.

He came back out a moment later with a bottle of grappa and two short, stubby glasses, which he put on the table made out of a piece of slate sitting atop some piled-up milk crates. The bottle of pure alcohol that Lenny kept in the freezer sweated onto the natural stone as we pounded back our first shot of the 180-plus-proof gold.

I explained the whole story from beginning to end, and explained to him the trouble that I thought I was in with this clown Staten.

"George Staten is old money, Elliot, and his wife is a loudmouthed, crusading whore. My grandfather had to fight him and his father to keep this place back in the mid-'90s, when the economy was just starting to open its eyes again. They wanted to take it from him. The two of them tried to bully him out of here 'cause he was Italian. Once the boys up on the hill and some of my grandfather's lifelong friends who still have big family-run businesses in the area caught wind of their bullshit, the Statens backed off."

"I don't think he's going to back off this one," I said.

"I remember a few years back—shit, it's probably been ten years now—this buddy of mine I went to school with was doing his wife."

"Who, Staten's wife?" I asked, a little confused.

"Yeah, Staten. My buddy told me that George knew and didn't care, because he was out porking anything that had a heartbeat. That's why this shit you're telling me doesn't surprise me in the least. These people are fucked up." Lenny put back another hard mouthful.

"It would be easier to kill the motherfucker! It's one thing to go out and find stupid women to sleep with you, but a kid? Staten is no better than that asshole Eddie G., who's running all this bad shit. I actually wouldn't be surprised if our fearless rep wasn't somehow in bed with that maggot Gomez!"

Lenny leaned over the armrest of his chair and pinched off the dead mums from leftover stock that hadn't sold during spring. "Not to get off the subject, but what do you think of these cement figures?" Lenny pointed to at least a dozen different garden birdbaths, waterfalls, and statues.

"I like them, Len."

"Listen, Elliot, you have to straighten this shit out. I don't know how, but I know that one way or another, you'll do it."

We both stood up and finished our glasses of booze. I stepped down onto the old, crooked brick sidewalk that led back to my car, and thanked Lenny for letting me bend his ear.

"Anytime, Elliot. I'll see you soon."

Slightly buzzed and a few notches calmer than when I'd shown up, I got into my car, feeling loose and stupid, but headed to the station anyway, ready to face what I had coming to me.

When I got to the station, I headed right to my desk and got started on my report. "The sooner I'm done, the better," I whispered under my breath.

I fantasized about finishing the whole bottle of Lenny's grappa and then smashing the bottle right over Staten's cheap twenty-five-cent head, right in front of his ugly wife.

Miranda walked up to my desk with a very serious manner and took me out of my daydream. "Elliot, I just want you to know that Stephanie has definitely had sex in the last twelve hours, and it was extremely rough and abusive." She pulled over a chair and sat down across from me.

"Any chance of Staten giving up his DNA?"

"Are you kidding me? He's already gone. His lawyer was here ten minutes after he arrived, threatening to sue the police department if we didn't release him."

"This dick is going to get off, isn't he? This is fucking ridiculous. He's having sex with a minor, for God's sake."

"Elliot, I hate to say this to you, but until you have court-worthy, concrete evidence, I would just let this go and play the 'I'm under a lot of stress' game."

"Is that what you would do?" I questioned her with a smug upper lip.

She got up and put the chair back. "What good is it if you're not here to help anyone at all?"

"Miranda, wait a minute." I stood up and leaned over, grabbing her arm. "I'm sorry. Thanks for looking out for me."

She turned and gave me a smile, letting me know that she was on my side, before disappearing around the corner.

I finished my report after the third rewrite, making sure that I didn't leave anything out. I climbed up a couple of floors to hand my report to Major Sullivan. I knocked on his open door and looked directly at him.

He looked up from his paperwork and waved me in. "Shut the door, Elliot, and sit down, please." He removed his reading glasses and pointed to the chair in front of his desk.

I held out my report and waited for him to grab it. "It's all there, Major."

He read it while I sat quietly, looking at him for a reaction.

"Is this a hundred percent accurate?" he asked.

"Yes, it is, sir. Everything happened exactly the way that report reads."

"IID wants me to suspend you while they investigate what happened this morning. They also talked to the DOC earlier about Raymond Chavez."

"Raymond Chavez? Who's that?"

"Yeah, he's the guy you beat in the middle of the street the other night."

"Oh, sorry, I didn't know his name." It wasn't worth hiding anything at that point. "What about him?"

"There's video footage of you wailing on him and then pulling out your piece."

I took Miranda's advice and played the game, trying to get anywhere but booted from Dicks. "Major, I've been under a lot of stress lately. For God's sake, my fiancée is a vegetable because of these thugs."

"Listen, Elliot, you're a good cop, and your service record before all this started is clean. If we play it their way, things will be much smoother for everyone. Take a week off without pay. Let's puff up IID's and Representative Staten's heads a bit, and maybe they'll go away. In the meantime, I'll work on a report about the recent stress you've been under. Trust me, kid, I don't want to do this, but I have no choice."

"I understand that I've put you in a shitty spot, sir."

Sullivan came around his desk. We shook hands and walked out of his office, and parted ways at his door.

I texted Sean to find out what his twenty was, so I could tell him the news. I made my way down the hall to hit the stairwell and got a text back from Sean that he was with Jimmy in his office.

"Hey, Elliot, where you been?" Jimmy asked.

"I'm officially suspended." I threw my hands up and glanced over at Sean, who was looking at the floor, not surprised by the news.

"Anything I should know before I leave the building?"

"Actually, yes," Jimmy said. "Some witnesses traveling on an overpass saw those two kids lose control of their car last night after an incident of road rage between them and another car. So Sean and I looked at the traffic cameras that shoot the incoming southbound traffic. Roughly ten minutes after the time these people claim they witnessed the deadly crash, look what comes rolling through."

I looked at the black-and white-shot of the highway Jimmy had pointed to on his screen. The slow-motion clip revealed a big, fancy Mercedes that looked just like Eddie G.'s ride.

"What bridge was this taken from?" I asked.

"The overpass lies roughly twelve miles south of the crash. The witnesses can't tell us what kind of car was involved with this particular incident, because it was dark and happened way too fast."

Sean paused the video, trying to see anything that might help identify the vehicle: the license plate, distinguishing marks, stickers, or maybe just Eddie's ugly mug framed behind the glass.

"Anything more on the explosion at Eddie's house?" I asked.

"Just that it was C-4 that blew the van," Sean said. "Oh, and they found traces of chicken broth or gravy at the back door."

Jimmy took a bite from a jelly stick that had been resting in his coffee. "Eddie lost a lot of guys this past week. You gotta know he's next."

"That'd probably be the best thing that could happen. Maybe then Elliot would stop getting in trouble." Sean looked at me with sarcasm written all over his face.

I winced. "Come on, man, that's a low blow."

"I'm just looking out for you. I don't wanna see you lose your job."

"I know. Neither do I. But I have to do what I feel is right. After all, why the hell did I become a cop in the first place?"

We all just stared at one another for a while, not knowing what to say.

"Not to change the subject, guys," Jimmy said, breaking the silence, "but I took it upon myself to look into Blake a little closer. "I called a doctor—a psychologist." He shuffled through some papers until he found what he'd been looking for. "Here it is, a Dr. Sweet."

"Is he here in Providence?" I asked.

"No, Florida. Walton County, actually. The VA released Blake three months after getting home from Vietnam, and then he started to see this shrink. According to Dr. Sweet, he never missed an appointment for five years. Then one day he just stopped showing up. Quit cold turkey, just like that."

I raised an eyebrow. "Five years straight? That's a long time."

"Dr. Sweet, who sounds like he's in his eighties, wouldn't release any information on Blake, but did say that he was unfit to be mixed in with general society." Jimmy put down the paper and looked at Sean and me with mixed emotions.

"I met the guy at the airport," I said. "He seems pretty sharp to me."

"Yeah, well, thirty-plus years and a family inheritance can heal a lot of wounds," Sean interjected.

"Wounds from wars never heal." I thought of my own scars that still itched in the night and sometimes bled. "Did you ever find a photograph of Blake? Or, for that matter, Steve Krasson?" I knew that somehow those guys were linked together somewhere along the line.

Jimmy shook his head. "Nope, no record of anything."

"I've had it!" I said. "I'm going home. I'm tired of banging my head against the wall." I looked at my watch, which read 5:50, and got up to leave for my mandatory vacation.

I walked up the stairs and left the building that I spent more time in than my own home. I glanced over at the abandoned house that was the start of my attempt at putting this crazy puzzle together. Everything had escalated so fast, especially after Megan got shot.

I almost walked right by my car. They were going to have to come pick it up if they wanted it, because I was driving it home.

Chapter 27

I pulled onto Washington Street as I passed the front of the police station, driving parallel with the southbound traffic on I-95. I looked down on the traffic while stopped at a red light and spotted a 1966 AC Cobra cruising down the highway with a rumble that I could hear over the four lanes of congestion. The two-seater pulled away and disappeared while I sat idle at the light in front of the station.

The light finally turned green, and I laid on the horn as I looked at the woman in front of me who was gabbing away on her cell phone, unaware that she was not the only one in the world. I went around her as she blew her horn back at me with her middle finger straight up in the air, and got on the highway in the hope of spotting the Cobra.

Traffic was heavy, making it difficult to catch up to and actually put eyes on the lightweight power plant. The needle on my speedometer rose and fell as I rode with the flow of traffic, which was bumper-to-bumper and very erratic. I read the lanes, scanning across, up, down, and diagonal as I came out of Thurber's Avenue, but couldn't get a fix on what I was looking for.

Cruising through Warwick, I approached the 95-to-295 split, where the highway climbed up a slight slope around the 117 exit, giving me a wider and longer reach on what I was hoping to grab onto. I scanned through the rows, across and forward, until I finally put my eyes on the Cobra stretching its legs roughly a quarter of a mile up in the left lane.

I lost the '66 again as the highway leveled off and the rows disappeared one by one, until there was just the car in front of me.

~~~

Grace and Steve pulled up to a hidden entrance that lay off the road. She put the car into park and unclipped her seatbelt. The sun had just disappeared, putting the sky in between shows. Grace took advantage of the intermission and leaned over and kissed Steve on his forehead. She looked into his eyes and told him that she loved him.

Filled with Grace's love and devotion, Steve grabbed her and held her close. He held a handful of her hair and grabbed the back of her neck as he gave her a passionate kiss that cut into the beginning of the sky's second performance. Their lips pulled apart as the second show rolled in, exposing the night's brilliant colors.

"I love you, Grace, so much." Steve ran his rough, oversized hand down the contour of her face.

He shut the passenger door and walked to the trunk, looking in every direction to make sure there was no one around the lonesome area they had chosen. He pulled up the trunk, lifted out his bag, and gaited off across the road as the trunk slowly closed. He stepped off the pavement and down the grass gully that lay a few feet below the grade of the road. Before diving into the world that cut him with love and hate, he turned and gave Grace a grin with his eyes, and then he disappeared.

Grace put the window up and pulled all four tires back onto the pavement, rolling away quietly under an intricately painted sky that reflected the subtleties of what was to come.

She turned on the car stereo, which powered up the compact disc player. The screen flashed in its cool blue display as the disc loaded and filled the car with nostalgia and sadness. She crept back into civilization with her eyes wide open, driving through the storm of memories until she broke down in tears and found it hard to stay in the lines. Reflections of all the yesterdays got tossed around as she sat in the now, heading toward sixty years old, a reality that bit into her and wouldn't let go.

~~~

Steve moved through a similar but rougher terrain as his knees cried out along with the dozens of injuries that called to him from over the years. He sat high atop the cliffs, keeping the ocean a pool below, playing it safe just in case someone was watching and maybe hunting him.

He lay down when he reached his destination, a piece of ledge split in half that shot out of the ground. Steve rummaged in his bag and pulled out a case that he opened on the flat ledge behind him. He put the two-piece long-range weapon together and then rested it between the cleft in the stone, giving him not only cover but a nice steady spot to unleash his last kill.

Steve zoned in on Eddie's home, made a few last-minute calculations and applied them to his weapon, and then he lay back and caught what was left of the sky for the night. Its colors hugged the horizon as the richness pulled out, leaving only faint hues and a memory of what had just been so predominant.

The skyline, day or night, talked to Steve and reached inside him, sometimes petting his ego and other times ripping his fucking heart out, while he sat powerless to it all.

He closed his eyes and took in a whiff of the cool ocean air as dusk set in and all remnants of the sun faded away. Steve looked down a pathway that cut a diagonal line away from where he rested, worn from general foot traffic over the years. The thin, tall grass that ran along the area swayed with the cross breezes, creating illusions that crossed the connections in Steve's head like a thick and heavy drug.

Eddie's sensor lights kicked on in the distance, blinding Steve with their brilliance.

~~~

Steve hears footsteps before a bright flashlight smashes him in the face. He is pulled up out of his hiding spot and beaten by two North Vietnamese soldiers. It's late 1969, and he has only a few months to go. He recently heard through the grapevine that Blake's broken platoon left the country three weeks ago, which gave him some type of sign that maybe his time with this war was almost up.

The two North Vietnamese soldiers take his sniper rifle and tell him that he is going to die by his own weapon. They drag him down a dark path with the pistol and his sniper rifle pressed to his back and head. The one on his left keeps pulling and tugging on Steve's damaged ear, bringing the soldier closer and closer to number one on his shit list.

They explain to Steve in broken English that they are taking him to an underground tunnel where he will be executed in front of enemy eyes, alone and surrounded by hate.

Steve reaches down inside his beltline and into his groin area while the two soldiers argue about who's going to pull the trigger and take his life. He grabs his silent weapon that the two nighttime sweepers failed to find. In one sweeping motion, he pulls out the double-edged blade and buries it into the closer man's tailbone. The man yelps and drops to the ground, paralyzed from the pain. Steve pulls out the buried knife and rolls into the thick green jungle, disappearing off the moonlit path.

The unharmed soldier, holding the pistol, fires into the shadows as images displayed by the moonlight and vegetation play tricks on him. He empties the clip on the .45-caliber and starts to run up the thin, overgrown path, leaving his partner holding his back and clenching his teeth from the pain. He runs with fear and tosses the empty pistol, which gets swallowed up by the jungle grass and overpowering bamboo.

The soldier branches to the right and runs into a fork in the path, where Steve's dagger flies through the air and into his neck. Knocked off his feet, he falls backward, holding the handle of the knife. Steve Krasson fills up his whole world and pulls out what was actually keeping the soldier from bleeding out.

Blood rises off the enemy's neck as Steve holds the dagger that was issued to him by the CIA in the spring of '68. The soldier quickly bleeds out and gurgles his last breath before going completely limp. Steve rolls him off the path and out of sight, and then he hears echoes of the other soldier's cries for help.

He sprints down the path, moving toward the screams begging for someone to come and rescue him. Steve dives on the man and covers his cries for help with his hand while grabbing a handkerchief out of his pocket to stuff in his mouth.

Now that the man can't make any more noise, Steve asks him if he had fun as he returns the favor, twisting and yanking on the man's ears. Steve grabs his knife, points the blade toward the sky, and smashes the soldier's front teeth out with the butt of the handle. The handkerchief in his mouth quickly turns red as blood pools up and overflows, running down the sides of his face.

Steve then turns the knife around and pushes his head to the side. The man struggles with everything he has left in him, but loses as Steve buries the steel in the soldier's ear until the handle bottoms out on his lobe. The body jumps up for a second and then lies back down, lifeless, as Steve pulls out the bayonet-style knife and wipes the blade on his sleeve.

He pushes the man into a thick patch with his foot and then picks up his rifle from the ground, throws it over his shoulder, and disappears back into the jungle, never to be seen by the enemy again.

~~~

Steve grabbed some almonds out of his bag for a small snack as he returned from the vicious flashback. After taking a few moments to watch the ocean and steady himself, he took a quick peek to see what Eddie was doing. He knew he probably wasn't going to get a clear shot of Eddie until morning, but he wouldn't sleep, hoping that Eddie would sleepwalk into his yard or skinny-dip in the pool under the moonlight with the other two freaks. Taking him out at night was what Steve wanted, but he knew that it was all up to luck.

~~~

Traffic was heavy between the lights on Route 4, but thinned out at the Jamestown Bridge exit. The tires on my car squealed around the half circle as I tried to catch up with my prey that I'd followed on a hunch. I neared the bottom of the exit and dropped it down by burying the pedal and tacking the engine up to its limit. I shot out of the hole, keeping my foot to the floor while pushing up the hill on Route 138. I started picking up speed on the downward slope toward the bridge and saw the

Cobra slip under the North Kingstown overpass.

I was closing in on the green dream car when the driver looked in his mirror, spotted me, and dropped down a gear, chirping the tires and waking up the engine that was pushing almost six hundred horses. When it was just a few car lengths ahead of me, the Cobra leapt up and instantly matched my downhill momentum until the incline of the bridge pulled it out from under me. The Cobra took a five-car lead and turned it into a disappearing act. I climbed to the peak, frustrated that I wasn't going to have an eyeball on this tiny jet by the time I got to the halfway mark and onto the Jamestown side of the bridge.

"Who the fuck is driving this car, and why are they running from me?" I said to myself out loud while looking at my eyes in the rearview mirror.

When I finally got to the top, where I had a full view of the island and the roadway below, the Cobra was nowhere in sight. I pulled my foot off the gas pedal and coasted down the second half of the bridge. The needle rolled back counterclockwise to a safer speed, pissing in my wound that I'd been smoked and had lost my objective.

If I'd been smart, I would've turned around and gone home, leaving the thought of going to Eddie's to my imagination, but I couldn't fight off my curiosity and intuition that were calling to me from the south side of the island.

I veered off the main drag that led to the Newport Bridge and stopped at the main artery that split the island in half. Major Sullivan's and Sean's voices pulled at me from the left, telling me to get back on the bridge and get my suspended ass home. I looked to the right, where no particular person or face called to me, but where something had set off my instincts and taken over my mind.

"Fuck it!" Letting the unknown tongue control my next move, I turned the wheel to the right and put on my headlights.

I bolted up the center roadway, used mainly by islanders, with what was left of the sunset gleaming off the car. I passed by a small bait-and-tackle shop near an open marsh where natural beauty took best in show by a long mile.

~~~

The unmarked stomped past the car and driver that had walked away from him back on the bridge, unable to observe the stick he'd been chasing as it bled into the shadows and sat well below the little natural light that was left.

The wide tires of the Cobra crunched down across the peastone driveway that it had backed into. Its driver, wearing a cap and fur-collared leather coat, feathered out the clutch and proceeded gingerly in the same direction as the cruiser.

~~~

"Hello?" I answered the private number that called me as I approached the ocean on Main Street.

"Elliot, it's Jimmy," he said with a quiet voice. "I'm calling from my personal phone."

"What's up, Jimmy?" I asked, confused by his call, and made a left.

"Listen, I'm telling you this and then shredding what I'm about to read you." I could hear him light up a cigarette and blow out the smoke across the mouthpiece.

"Okay, what is it?"

"Jack was in Vietnam, right?"

"Just get to where you're going, Jimmy." I sat with a pit in my stomach, not wanting to play twenty questions. I was just minutes away from Eddie's house.

"Okay. Jack was in Blake's platoon." He took another long drag from the cigarette to help calm his nerves.

"What? Are you sure?" I thought there had to have been a mistake.

"Well, not in the same unit, but close enough that they knew each other. Both of them returned home wounded in battle just a couple of months shy of their second tour. Blake, obviously, much worse than Jack."

"Why wouldn't Jack tell me that?" I asked myself aloud.

"It really doesn't mean anything," Jimmy said nervously. "I mean, it sort of does . . . Not that Jack is killing people, just that maybe he didn't want to talk about old memories or rat on a fellow brother. I don't know. I just thought you should know." Jimmy treaded the waters carefully, knowing how close Jack and I were.

"This stays between us, Jimmy. Not even Sean." I wanted to keep things quiet for now, knowing that a black-and-white jury could not ingest this gray information without good litigation.

"Like I said, it's going through the shredder as soon as I get back inside."

"Maybe you're right, Jimmy. Old, painful memories." I got lost for a moment as my mind went blank. "Listen, I'll talk to you later. Thanks again for the heads-up on the info."

"No problem. I'll call if I find anything else."

I put my phone away, thinking back on Jack's reaction to Grace as she had walked down the staircase at VBG Properties, and their good-bye while I'd been fixed on the picture of Blake's platoon.

I also thought about how Jack had moved my car that day at the hospital, and about that piece of shit with his head split wide open who had tried to kill Megan. It just didn't make sense. After all the years and all the time spent with Jack, you'd think I would know something like this about him.

I pulled onto the road that Eddie lived on and shut my lights off, staying a fair distance away from his property.

~~~

Steve got to his rifle and pointed it at Eddie's entrance gate, which needed total rehabilitation from the explosion. He saw Detective Frantallo get out of his unmarked and stand between the pillars, looking at the damage and aftermath of what he had only heard about through the grapevine. Steve dialed in his high-powered scope and could see that Elliot was taken aback by the damage as he looked everything over and tried to create a visual in his own mind of what had happened.

Steve Krasson was very interested in the young detective, and watched his every move. Elliot stepped over the property line and walked onto the driveway, which made Steve quickly pivot the rifle to Eddie's house, waiting to see the panic that would ensue when the driveway sensor went off.

Eddie came charging down the hallway with a revolver in his hand. Steve put his sights back on the detective. He admired Elliot, but he was puzzled as to why he would just mouse in through the big front gateway that still had Eddie twitching.

"What the fuck are you doing here?" Eddie yelled out as he shoved the front door open in a storm of rage that burned up his face.

Steve watched as Eddie turned on all the lights and walked outside with a dog on either side of him. His pistol was stuffed in the waistline of his cargo shorts, covered by the colorful polo he'd thrown on when he first heard the sensor go off. The dogs stayed tight by Eddie's side, following his commands and watching every move the Providence detective made.

Chapter 28

"I really don't think he's gonna push the envelope after you just saved his life," the driver of the Cobra said.

Steve looked out at the bay. "We could really use a kid like this, but he needs a little lesson on patience."

They both drew off the short smokes they had picked for tonight's victory kill.

"Fuck it, then," the driver said. "You know as well as I that he's tucked in waiting for us. Let's see what point he's at in his life." A grin spread across his face, knowing that the George Staten incident could be the cavity that made Elliot quit candy.

~~~

"So, after all the trouble you're in, you still went down there?" Denise sat on the edge of the couch that had been her bed for the past week, blown away by my story from the night before.

"I had to," I said. "I just couldn't leave it alone."

"Okay, so you pulled up and walked down his driveway. Then what happened?"

"He came out as pissed as anyone could be and said, 'What are you doing on my property, cop?'"

~~~

His large, protective Akitas bared their teeth, sensing their master's tone.

"I heard about your little mishap and figured I would come check it out for myself," I said.

"What, do you think you're funny, pig?"

"Nothing about any of this is funny. I got suspended from my job because of you and the mutts you hang out with."

"What the hell are you talking about *my* fault?"

"Selling a minor to George Staten. Come on, man, drugs are one thing, but screwing around with kids? I busted Staten's nose this morning for screwing a little girl who you're making money off of, and now I'm the bad guy! I'll tell ya, you must have no conscience whatsoever."

"I can't control everything my guys do, and as far as that girl is concerned, she don't have a shot anyway. If it wasn't for me, she'd probably be dead in the gutter."

"That's why you and Staten will eventually go down. Neither of you give a shit about anyone but yourselves. One day, one of you assholes will step in the wrong pile of shit and get what you have coming to you." I backed up slowly and got closer to the road, knowing this loose cannon could blow as the conversation soured.

"I bet you think you're going to be the one that's gonna find that magic pile, don't you?" Eddie grabbed his chest and burst out laughing.

"It's just a matter of time before you're behind bars, Eddie, or dead."

"That's going to be a neat trick," Eddie declared to me as he pulled out a gun.

"Oh, so now you're going to kill me?"

"The way I see it, I'd be stupid if I didn't. Look over here. Check it out. The headlines will read *Obsessive Providence Cop Attacks Businessman on His Property in Jamestown After Being Suspended for Knocking Out a State Rep Earlier That Day*." Eddie talked with stars in his eyes while he painted the news flash with his other hand. He pulled back the hammer on the stainless six-shooter. "I'll call the cops after I call my lawyer, as you bleed out where my friends and lover just died because of you! Then my lawyer will pin the explosion on you because of your heroic military bullshit background." Eddie cackled and stiffened his arm, readying for the night's kill.

Smack!

Eddie's head thrust sideways, and blood sprayed out of his head like the mist from a juicy orange as he fell to the ground. The dog to his left let out a whimper while he struggled to get out from underneath Eddie's body. Ironically, it looked as if Eddie's plans for me had been someone else's plans for him.

I looked up in the darkness to the enormous patch of land that lay peaceful and quiet next to Eddie's lot. I heard crickets and could see squat as I scanned the trees and underbrush that scribed out a definite contrast between Fort Wetherill and the sky above.

~~~

"Elliot, are you okay?" Denise asked as I pulled up a chair and grabbed Megan's hand.

"It just looked like she was listening to the story, like she could understand."

Silence drifted around the three of us as one of Megan's monitors beeped and the HVAC ceiling diffuser made a subtle roar. She lay in her bed, still not moving.

"Tell me the rest of what happened last night," Denise said.

~~~

The front door opened on Eddie's house, letting out screams of terror and sorrow that pushed me off the property and away from the professional hit that had taken place an arm's length away. Eddie's dogs sniffed and licked at him while a young man and woman came running out, howling with sadness.

I backed up over the property's pinstripe and ran back to my car, parked behind the stone wall. I opened my car door to call in this nightmare to the Jamestown Police Department, and heard a specific thunder roll my way. The rumble cut through the heaviness of the atmosphere as the intensity of my intuition coagulated, putting my sniffer back into the game.

I heard the roar of the Cobra take off in the immediate distance. I put my car in drive and hung my head out the window, trying to follow what I had already lost once that night. I took the shortest route back to the bridge and shot by the police station at better than a buck ten, and saw two marked cruisers all lit up on the opposite side of the guardrail. I drove up the wrong side of the road, then snapped a line and cut across the tollbooth threshold and back to the westbound double lane that shared asphalt with the arch that connected Jamestown with the mainland.

I slowed down and pulled over, rolled to a stop, and shut off the engine, hoping to hear the old muscle car driving my way. I knew that Eddie G. getting smoked was going to be big trouble for me, but I was glad the dirtbag was dead.

I grabbed my phone and called Sean. "Come on, pick up."

Sean answered on the first ring. "Hello?"

"Sean, it's me. Eddie just got taken out by our sniper friend." I bit into an apple that had been rolling around my car for the past few days.

"Are you kidding me?"

"No, I'm not. He's dead in his driveway." I kept my ears wide open, waiting to hear the thunderous side pipes of the '60s dream car.

"And let me guess, you were just strolling by eating an ice cream cone when it happened."

"Ha-ha. I came down because I was following a hunch. I told you that Eddie was next. This whole thing was one big plan that I have to be cleared of, and the surveillance at his house should prove that."

Sean called Jimmy on the hard line while holding my call, and recited everything to him so he could get a jump on making a few phone calls to Jamestown PD.

"So where did Eddie get it?" Sean asked after hanging up with Jimmy.

"Right in the head. He actually never felt a thing." I thought back to Eddie's eyes as he was seconds away from pulling his own trigger and ending my life.

"I'll keep this quiet and buy you as much time as I can, but you know, at some point, they're going to finger you as a suspect and come after you."

"Yeah, I know. Just remember, they should be barking up Staten's tree now, not mine. But like I said, make sure someone gets that surveillance clip at Eddie's. That will prove I didn't do a thing wrong, except maybe trespass."

"All right. I'll talk to you soon, Elliot. Try to stay out of trouble!"

"Okay, thanks, Dad." I hung up the phone to the sound of Sean's laughter.

~~~

"That's when I called you to check in but hung up right away," I said.

"Oh yeah, I remember," Denise said. "You talked for like ten seconds and then disappeared. *Well*, are you going to finish? I have to hear how this ends."

"Okay, sorry. Still trying to ingest it all. So I looked at the bridge. Both lanes were empty, and it was well lit. I remember taking a second to appreciate the quiet structure. That's when the Cobra tore by me."

~~~

"Holy shit!" I dropped my phone on the passenger's seat. The smell of raw fuel knocked at my palate as it lingered in and around my head and woke me up for another chase.

I spilled out onto the road with everything I had and made it to the bridge within seconds. I saw the Cobra step onto North Kingstown as I reached the top of the bridge and tried not to lose sight or reach of the perp who had just saved my life. I followed the car, but this time with ease as we punched down the highway, staying at a steady hundred. Something inside me held a distance between license plates, almost as if I were following and not chasing after him.

The night's events got tossed around with ideas and speculation as my inner voice told me Jack was somehow involved in all of this. I thought back in my mind to the past week, to Jack's involvement and his reactions, to what had seemed like typical bits and pieces of what normal reflexes or conversation would be. Now, in the present, with the recoil hitting me square between the eyes, my visions appeared much different from what I had experienced in the moment. Maybe being ignorant to the facts is just as bad as being blind.

The green highway signs in their reflective frames popped up and disappeared as I sped past, along with the lane lines as they were eaten up by the hood of the car. Hanging upside down in my cave, staring at my drab expression, wasn't going to get me past the fact that Jack was possibly driving the Cobra that was cutting a path back to the city.

The Big Blue Bug watched over us as we steamed by on the lower northbound tear of I-95. With no directional, the Cobra swept three lanes and just missed the Jersey barrier as it jumped onto the Point Street Bridge exit. I followed suit but skimmed the barrier, adding one more battle scar to the abused unmarked Crown Vic as I skipped across the pavement and followed the leader, who was heading right toward my neighborhood.

"I can't believe this!" I announced inside the empty car as the Cobra made a left and then quick right, pulling onto a street that made my seat hot. I stepped on the brake with two feet.

My throat started to swell from the denial that was pumping straight from my gut and onto the street. The Cobra came to a rolling stop right in front of Jack's front steps, and I stopped roughly a car length behind, leaving my lights on. I put my car in park and left it running while I stepped out and stopped halfway to the cherry red taillights of the '66.

The passenger and driver stood up and faced me as they climbed out of the shadows and met me somewhere in the middle of the empty space that lay between us. Jack and Blake stood in front of me, leaving me speechless but somehow not surprised.

Jack cleared his throat. "Elliot, I think it's about time you met my friend Steve Krasson."

~~~

Megan's grip pulled me away from the previous night's story.

"Denise, come here," I said. "Megan's eyes are open."

"Oh my God!" Denise stood up in shock. "Megan, can you hear me?"

Megan blinked and smiled as she finally broke through the coma. She looked at me with her kind eyes and a soft smile that swept all the dirt off my front doorstep and onto the sidewalk below. I turned to Denise, who was crying with happiness as she sat down across from me and took hold of Megan's other hand.

A small breeze cleared the sidewalk of all the remnants as I shut the front door and turned off the light, wondering what would show up on my doorstep tomorrow.

Author's Note

As I lay in the hospital on a gurney watching my wife and mother walk away, I turned my head thinking of the neck surgery that I was about to have and the liability release I had just signed only minutes ago. The damage to the disc in my neck was so severe that I was at risk of losing the use of my right arm. The last thing I needed was to have my neck cut open with a recovery time of six months or more. After 20 years of hard work and building up my plumbing business, I was afraid I would lose everything.

My right arm was failing so badly that I couldn't even hold a wrench, so you guessed it, I hit a wall! When I woke up on the third floor of Miriam Hospital feeling like I had swallowed a glass full of beach sand, my doctor arrived announcing that my surgery had been a success and that I would be able to go home as soon as the neck drain stopped leaking. Several days later I left the hospital wearing a restrictive neck brace that would remain in place for months.

When I arrived home, I settled on the couch in front of the TV and that's where I stayed for the next three months. Netflix movies and television series occupied most of my time. But when staring at the ceiling had taken the upper hand, I knew it was time for me to do something else. Everything I was accustomed to doing was against doctor's orders. In an instant like a sudden downpour, I decided to write a book. At first the idea seemed strange to me because I never had a free moment in the past 20 years to even think about writing a book. I owned dozens of wrenches but no typewriter or laptop, and if I did I wouldn't know how to turn them on.

Looking down at a pen and pad was also against doctor's orders. My only outlet was the one thing that was attached to my hip, literally and that was my iPhone 4. Using my phone I started to get my ideas down, reading bits and pieces of the story to my family and friends with dreams of someday finishing this manuscript. Some people thought that I was wasting my time but I was determined to put plumbing behind me and come out of this surgery an author. I pecked away tirelessly at the keyboard on my phone finishing *Exhale With Intent* in five months and 68,000 words later.

When I returned to work after seven months, I hit my head on a bulkhead tearing the ligaments in my neck. I was quickly out of work for thirteen months and able to concentrate on my story again. During this time, I talked to my lawyer, friends and family, and even others authors about how to proceed with my book. I found my editor through an author who is related to a friend of mine. When the editor read my manuscript and agree to work with me, I admit my smile touched both ears. Now I'm completely edited and ready to share my personal story with the one I wrote. I hope everyone enjoys my book *Exhale With Intent* and is ready for the prequel.

Thank you.

Author Bio

Born in Rhode Island, I have spent my adult career as a plumber and a contractor. In December 2012, I was forced to have neck surgery. Though difficult and painful, it opened my eyes to the world of self-creation, and I wrote Exhale with Intent while recovering. I have also started the prequel to Exhale with Intent and have begun painting on the side. My art has been accepted by a gallery in Putnam, Connecticut, where I am presently showing my work. I believe that my passion for movies and my sense of feeling every emotion related to every visual detail has enabled me to push forward, not only as an artist in the usual sense, but as an artist who wants to feel and project the truth about what I'm saying. When not working, I spend time with my wife, family, and friends, who are all very close to my heart.

Made in the USA
Middletown, DE
13 April 2016